GUESTS

Kealan Patrick Burke

Originally appeared in GUESTS published by Suntup Editions

Elderlemon Press

ISBN: 9798366719049

guests

kealan patrick burke

"...one of the roles of man is to shut his eyes and keep them shut to see if he can continue into the night of his old age the dream curtailed in the night of his youth."

— Machado de Assis, *Dom Casmurro*

KEALAN PATRICK BURKE

1

I N THE END, IT WAS THE GODDAMN ROLLING PIN that did it. Until then, I'd somehow managed to hold it together through the phone calls and the preparations and the funeral and the procession of grim-faced well-wishers, few of whom I knew, and whose gravity I did everything to resist in case it smashed me against the concrete floor of my own grief. But I held on, nodding where appropriate, and probably on occasion, where it wasn't.

"So sorry for your loss, Mark."

"Thank you."

"She was a good woman."

"She was."

The density of empty words.

What I wanted to do was stare intently down into my grandmother's grave and demand she return. I know death is normal. For a moment, I forgot, or didn't care. This new reality pushed and pressed against me in a way that made my skin crawl and I wanted to be done with it. *I'm done, I'm done. You've had your fun.* I peered down into the earth and silently insisted she come back. But what would that have wrought? Grief is dishonest and irrational. It makes us believe we would do anything to restore the natural order as we perceive it, even though it is the very same order that extinguishes the ones we love. And should our wish be fulfilled and the dead return, we'd be left to answer for denying them their peace just so we could be spared the anguish.

"Don't go," I said to the woman already gone.

After, I endured the platitudes and ministerial affectations of the priest, and left in the back of a stranger's car, ferried home by some distant relative who hadn't existed before that day and would cease to exist tomorrow.

* * *

They say you never appreciate the beauty of a place until you leave it, the appeal only obvious in retrospect, but it was impossible not to be awed by the sheer immensity of the sea as our funereal sedan labored its way up Parchment Hill. They said the road would be closed to all but the plows and emergency vehicles soon, but even in good weather, that hill was treacherous: a steep and narrow incline barely wide enough to accommodate one vehicle, never mind two. If you were unfortunate enough to meet a truck coming against you, you had three options: pull off onto the thin strip of gravel on your right side by the sheer wall, reverse back the way you came until the road opened up, or plow through the shaky old guardrails and take the long but quick 400-foot drop into the patient sea.

The ocean was a heaving gray beast that day, the waves like shudders across its skin. A freighter looked like an ink stain on the horizon. It began to snow as I looked out through the fog of my own breath on the window, and it was as if my grandmother's death had drained the color from the world, my emotions as contained as the sea's own secrets, both of us in quiet turmoil and roiling beneath the surface.

And then I was at my grandmother's house where I had lived since the day the police came to my door to tell me that my parents hadn't taken the first two options on Parchment Hill.

Magda's house was distinguishable from the cluster of similar Cape Cods on Shoreline Road by the explosions of flowers, so ubiquitous and profuse, it was these and not the house that seemed the predominant feature, as if the building had been added as an afterthought. It stood in relief against the splayed denuded hands of the sycamore trees in the backyard. She'd been a fervent gardener, her thumb green enough to know the blooms that would, unlike the woman herself, survive the winter. Thus, while her neighbors' gardens looked appropriately barren as the first snow fell, Magda's remained vibrant. I couldn't remember the names of all the flowers, though because she had taken such great pride in her garden, there had barely been a day when she hadn't mentioned them. The Gloriosas had stuck because the word sounded like a spell from a fantasy book. So too did the black-eyed Susans, the Peter Pans, and the Johnny-Jump Ups. The rest I had

5

forgotten and that day, as I closed the wrought-iron gate behind me and made my way up the garden path, that made me sad in a way I find difficult to describe. There was not a single flower in that garden that did not summon the memory of my late grandmother's joy in attending to them, but joyful ghosts are still reminders of death.

Houses don't feel as empty if you know the person who lives in them will return. In the wake of a death, the silence is unique, and awful. It has a peculiar weight to it, like an immobile ghost there for the sole purpose of filling the vacuum its owner left behind. A shoddy impression. My grandmother's passing made the house unfamiliar despite it being my home. My footsteps sounded like a violation, my presence an affront in a sacred place. When, out of habit, my fingers alighted on things: a newel post, the kitchen table, the cupboard door, it felt as if it had grown a protective second skin. So enormous was her presence here, my grandmother's passing had rendered everything unfamiliar. I was twenty-two but might as well have been fourteen again in the wake of my parents' death: confused, alone, and in pain, with no idea what to do.

I tossed my phone on the table and fetched from behind her enormous cadre of colored glass jars of flour and rice and pastas, the small bottle of Irish whiskey Magda had assumed I didn't know was there. Then I brought it to the table and didn't bother with a glass. Still the tears wouldn't come. They hadn't come at the graveside either as I tossed a handful of crumbly dirt down into her grave because all I could think of was the sound it made as it hit the lid of the coffin. There was nothing peaceful about that sound. Hail against a window, stones against tin. It sounded hostile and echoed around inside the chambers of my skull long after I'd shaken the last hand, because I imagined her in there *hearing* it.

To my right stood the small portable black and white TV, a relic of a bygone era Magda used to watch her soap operas while cooking. I considered turning it on if only to break the silence, but then thought of how it would feel if one of those 'stories' happened to be on. I didn't think I'd ever again be able to hear the *Days of Our Lives* theme music without crumbling to pieces.

To my left, a tall pine cupboard stood against the wall by the door to the pantry. Like almost everything else in the house, Magda had had it longer than I'd been alive. Attached to its midsection was a retractable shelf, and on this shelf lay my grandmother's rolling pin. It, too, was old, and from where I sat, I saw there was a single thumbprint imprinted on flour on the roller. As evidenced by the pristine condition of the house even after she got sick, Magda had been fastidiously clean. She would have been annoyed to know she'd left even a smudge of flour in her wake. I considered getting up and wiping it off, but I couldn't do that no more than I'd been able to turn on the TV. Perhaps in whatever realm in which she now existed, she might have appreciated the gesture, or thought it callous. Or, and this I found most likely, she was dead and thus, incapable of thought at all. Whatever the case, my breath caught so suddenly, I almost choked on it. Startled, I sat back, the bottle in my hand, and tried to assess what had just happened to me. Gradually, the sense of tension spread like a hand down my throat, pushing further down until it was squeezing the breath from my lungs. My vision blurred. Desperately I looked around the kitchen for my grandmother who I knew must be there because that was how the proper world worked and saw nothing but shimmering ghosts spasming brokenly around the room.

I exhaled, and with it the tears and anguish finally broke free, pulsing out of me in merciless waves, leaving me a sobbing wreck at the kitchen table.

2

I COULDN'T STAY IN THE HOUSE. Perhaps the situation would change given time, but for the night at least, I needed to be away from there. Trouble was, there was a snowstorm on the way, and I had no place else to go, or rather, no place I wanted to be. A call from Naomi, arguably the only person left in my world I gave a damn about now that Magda was gone, changed my mind.

"Hey."

"Hey yourself," she said, sounding breathless.

"You okay?"

"It's freezing out here."

"You at work?"

"You say that like I'm ever anywhere else. I'm out behind the dumpsters. I snuck out here to call you, but I ended up having a cigarette with Sheri and she wouldn't stop going on about the new guy."

"What new guy? A new hire?"

"Off season? Yeah, right. The new guy she's dating."

I liked Sheri Milford. At fifty-six, the head of housekeeping was also something of a house mother for the rest of the staff.

Behind the veneer of her benevolent disposition and sly humor, however, was the unfinished story of an unhappy life. Truncated episodes emerged on rare occasions when she was feeling wistful, or down, or had one too many cocktails in The Ocean Room after work. There was an abusive ex-husband in there, a distant mother, a father with dementia, and an ongoing struggle with painkillers after the surgeries to fix her leg. These shadows seldom cast a pall on her, though, at least at the hotel, where she worked efficiently and tirelessly to keep her house in order.

"Let's hope this one's better than the last," I said.

"God, I hope so. How did today go?"

I fingered the bottle of whiskey. "I put my grandmother in a box and that box in the ground. I've had better days."

"Yeah, that was a dumb question. I'm sorry. I told you I'm shit when it comes to other people's grief. It's not that I don't feel awful, you get that right?"

"Of course. After today, I'm never offering my condolences again. It's all so...meaningless."

"I just don't know how to *be* is the thing," Naomi said. "Like, I'm really sorry she's gone, and I'm worried about you, but I don't know exactly what I'm supposed to say. 'Thoughts and prayers, bruh?'"

I smiled at that. "It's okay, really. It means a lot to me that you called. I'm glad you did."

"Yeah?"

"Yeah." And I meant it. I was always glad to hear from Naomi, even if it was usually *me* who didn't always know what to say. It had been that way since the first day I saw her. She'd transferred to my high school from Dayton, Ohio and unlike most people who react in quiet terror to new environments, Naomi seemed totally at ease as she took a seat in History class. It was that self-confidence, the perpetual hint of a smile, the alabaster skin and wavy auburn hair, and the look in her eyes that dared you to try and fuck with her at your own peril that made my heart skip a beat. The intervening years hadn't diluted that feeling at all. Every time I saw her, I felt short of breath.

"I'm sorry I couldn't make the funeral. Jessop was a dick about it, especially after I told him that all staff should have gone, him included."

"I'm sure he loved hearing that."

"He turned his big Tell-Tale Heart eye on me."

"Yikes."

"Followed it with that whole *responsibility to the guests* spiel we've all heard eight million times before."

"He has a point, though." I glanced at the rolling pin with that ghostly thumbprint, and then quickly looked away. "You couldn't just ditch the place for the afternoon, and besides, it would have been weird for me to have everyone there."

"*I* could have come, though, at the very least. I feel rotten that I didn't."

"I'm not sure I'd have wanted you there."

"Why?"

"It was a funeral. *I* almost didn't go, but Magda would have haunted me till the end of my days if I hadn't." I also hadn't

11

wanted Naomi to see me that broken and vulnerable. I might have told her things she'd rather not have heard.

Like the truth about how I felt about her.

She sighed. "I don't like that you had to be there by yourself. Were any of your family there?"

"Couple of people I recognized from Magda's photo albums. Nobody who meant much to me, though. Her son—my uncle— didn't show."

"Wow."

"Too busy wheeling and dealing in Dubai, apparently."

"Charming."

"Yeah, she didn't talk much about him. What she did say, wasn't good."

"Takes a special kind of asshole to miss his mother's funeral."

"They hadn't been close in many years. Not since she refused to bail him out when he got busted for dealing drugs in his late teens."

"Jesus. How have you never told me this?"

"Never came up."

"Well, I want to hear more about it sometime, but I should get back inside. Freezing my nips off out here. You still coming back on Monday?"

"Actually, I was thinking of heading that way now."

"Tonight? Why? Stay at home, for God's sake. Nobody should be here who doesn't have to be."

"I know, but I think I'd feel better there than here. For tonight at least."

"Well, it might *be* for the whole night. Jessop warned us we could get snowed in. The weather report backs him up. Anyone else would have sent us home and shuttered the place till the storm blows over, but not our dear Jessop. We're down to the skeleton crew and he's assigned us rooms already. Not sure he'll extend you the same courtesy though. You may end up on a couch in the lobby."

Or we could share, I thought of saying, but as with so many of the things that occurred to me to say to the girl with whom I was hopelessly and inconveniently in love, it would have been unfair, so I didn't. "Or the broom closet," I said instead.

"You thinking of taking a shift or just hanging out? I know Jessop's in a tight spot with Julia out on maternity and Rick's busted leg. He'd probably appreciate the help if you were willing to pitch in. We could use you in the bar. It's going to be busy and nobody else is willing to risk the drive."

"Sure. You want to mention it to him? I can get cleaned up and be there by five."

"Will do. He'll probably call to confirm."

"I doubt it. He doesn't talk to me if he can avoid it."

The delight in her voice warmed my heart. "Okay then, great. Aargh, I'm so excited. It'll be much more fun with you here. We can tear some shit up, yo."

"It'll be a night to remember," I said. *And it's going to be my last one.*

I don't think I made the decision until that moment, but I knew it was the truth. I was going to quit my shitty job and quit pretending I had even the slightest reason to stay, because the reality was that with Magda gone, there was nothing else to keep me here. Miriam's Cove was a ghost town, and it would smother me like it had my father, who had a headful of dreams crushed out of him in his youth, only to have everything else crushed in a car crash trying to go on vacation with his wife sixteen years later. You paid for trying to escape this dreamless town, just as I would.

In truth, I should have taken my grandmother up on her offer to pay my way through college when she'd offered. My future might have been very different if I had. But that old Irish pride had led me to refuse. That, and I don't think my grandmother really knew just how expensive it would have been. I couldn't have had it on my conscience if she'd ended up putting a second mortgage on her home just to keep me in wild parties. Instead, I took the job at The Windcrest Hotel, where the wages were dismal, the working conditions only marginally better, and the notion of advancement laughable. But on that fateful night at my dead grandmother's table in which I threw the dice and decided life was going to take me away from Miriam's Cove once and for all, I'd worked at the hotel for four years. And that was four years too many. There was no future in The Windcrest, no future with Naomi, thus, no future in Miriam's Cove. The truth was I'd stayed for the worst, most idiotic reason of all: a girl I would never have.

I realized it had been a moment since I'd said anything, but I could still hear the huff of Naomi's breathing.

"Hey, you still there?"

"Yeah," she said, "but I'm back inside, and if Jessop catches me…"

"You said tonight was going to be busy? Why, if the roads are going to close?"

"We had a booking today."

"Really? I'm surprised anybody's traveling."

"No kidding. But it gets better. It's a bunch of old folks."

"Veterans, or something?"

"Something. We'll be lucky if half of them don't croak before th—"

I winced on her behalf.

"Shit," she said. "Sorry."

I summoned a smile so she could hear it in my voice. "Go, before he catches you on the phone."

"Going. Gone. Bye."

KEALAN PATRICK BURKE

3

I WASN'T DRUNK BUT I ALSO DIDN'T TRUST myself to drive Magda's beat-up old Chevy Nova in the snow (or any other time, for that matter), so I called an Uber instead. He arrived fifteen minutes later, a friendly Middle Eastern guy who wanted to talk about the weather. After a few minutes of preamble, we lapsed into a silence that seemed to suit us both.

The snow was falling harder now, but without the power of the wind behind it, it hadn't yet graduated to a blizzard. I wasn't worried about getting home if the storm did what the weather report said it was going to. I assumed I could crash at the hotel, Jessop's objections notwithstanding, and if not, I could cadge a ride with whomever decided to brave the elements (and someone always did.) We were no strangers to winter storms, or the kinds of dumb decisions we sometimes had to make to get through them.

I'd started working as a waiter in the Windcrest not long after high school until (and truth be told, before) I was old enough to tend bar. Despite Magda's offer to finance my education, I needed to make real money and pay my own way. By giving me a home when my world collapsed and doting on me every day since, she had done way more than should ever have been expected, but rather unfairly, my dependence on her had started to feel

17

suffocating. She wouldn't be around forever, and without her, I worried I would spin out, which, despite my efforts and hers, proved prophetic. I was already coming apart, just not for the reasons I'd always thought. The hereditary albatross of alcoholism, perhaps, or the crushing weight of existential panic. I'd missed the most likely reason of all for everything to unravel: my grandmother's death.

I would need to see her lawyer in a few days. I expected he would tell me Magda had left me the house, the car, and maybe a small bit of money. If so, I planned to sell it all and move away from here as soon as I was able. If she didn't leave me a dime, I'd figure out a way to make it on my own.

There was, quite simply, nothing else left for me to do, and often, that's the only motivation you need to make a dramatic change.

* * *

"Here we go," said the driver, the engine idling. My phone buzzed in my pocket to let me know our transaction was complete. Beyond him, through the haze of snow, stood the hotel in all its wintry grandeur.

Built in 1927 by a British architect named Thomas Windcrest, the enormous Queen Anne Victorian had always seemed out of place in Miriam's Cove, a small town full of Cape Cods with a population of a little less than five hundred. Despite being a stone's throw from Cape Elizabeth, The Cove had never seen the kind of tourism to justify a sprawling hotel and indeed, for many years it served more as an austere winter home for the architect and his family, who split their time between The Cove and his ancestral home in Leeds. Of his many properties, The Windcrest was the architect's least elaborate and therefore least celebrated, which might explain why, over time, his interest in it waned. It had never yielded much profit, and the town hadn't warmed to him or his wife and two children, partly because they were *from away*, mostly because Windcrest had insisted on using his own laborers to construct the house rather than hiring local tradesmen, as was his custom. Mainers are warm people, but when slighted, and in the absence of reparation or apology, can hold a grudge for generations. Though Windcrest was a stoic and stolid man, he grew tired of his neighbors making him jump through hoops for supplies and overcharging for repairs (his snobbery apparently didn't extend to common maintenance work), and after World War II ended, with architects in high demand for government and federal projects, Windcrest departed The Cove for the last time.

The current owners were Tory and Mason Cross, an interior designer and real estate developer respectively. Their approach was very much hands-off, which suited the staff, because whenever they did appear for the occasional "seasonal lunch" (impromptu inspection), they were pious and aloof. It was clear they had little interest in the place beyond whatever cachet it earned them at their various clubs. It was one of over a dozen properties they owned and thus, represented little more than a few pages in an account book. The people tasked with maintaining it mattered little. It didn't help

19

that The Crosses brought with them an air of numbered days. They were frequently overheard discussing all the ways in which the land could be better utilized, the loamy shorefront locale making it an ideal place for a golf course.

I stepped out of the car, the snow needling my face, and dug my hands into my pockets against the biting chill. Once upon a time, there had been a wide expanse of gravel here where the guests parked their cars. Now an asphalt parking lot three times the size of the hotel spread from its doors, stopping a few yards shy of the thin strip of beach. Unlike Windcrest, the Crosses were not dissuaded by realistic projections of seasonal occupancy. To them, if it looked grand and ostentatious enough, people would seek it out. They were wrong of course, the brunt of the tourism trade lured away by the aesthetic pleasures of Cape Elizabeth and Bar Harbor. Now, the oversized and mostly empty lot only underscored the owners' detachment from the economic reality of the region.

That day, there were only four cars in the lot, what Magda used to call "a Sunday crowd." Lording over it all, stood the hotel itself. Despite the renovations and rebuilding, its age was evident in the way the gables seemed to sag and the tall decorative chimneys to lean just so. Over the years, more attention had been given to the lower levels of the building so that now, from the upper stories to the finials, the paint seemed more faded, the scalloped slate more worn. The Crosses enthusiasm for their own project had dulled since the acquisition and it showed. From where I stood, it looked like a squat giant huddled in on itself, no line true, no angle unchallenged by the gravity of age. The double hung windows seemed at odds with each other, though this may have been an illusion aided by the flaking paint and bowing frames. Decades of saltwater abrasion had worn the skin from the hotel's face and left it raw and exposed to the elements. It radiated sadness and vulnerability. Barring intervention, it would not survive another decade.

I watched my reflection approach in the glass of the heavy double doors.

Hand on the icy brass handle, I had the queerest thought and with it came an inexplicable feeling of dread almost enough to make me turn and try to flag down the Uber. *Go home. This was a mistake.*

But my ride was already gone, the snow falling quietly in the parking lot behind me.

KEALAN PATRICK BURKE

4

I'D HOPED HE WOULDN'T BE, BUT PETE LEWIS was working the reception desk. He raised a hand in greeting when he saw me enter the lobby, his face warmed by a genuine smile. "Look what the polar vortex blew in!"

At twenty-three, he was a year older than me, smarter and better-looking, and liked by everyone except Jessop, who didn't like anyone. Tall and well-built, with a mop of hair dyed the color of summer sand, he was funny, perpetually good-humored, and nigh-on impossible to dislike unless you harbored a natural enmity for good people. I didn't hate him, but not a day went by that I didn't wish I could. It would have made me feel better to find some fault I could latch onto, to expose him as a pretender, a fraud, a fake. I fantasized about uncovering some sinister truth he had kept from us all, of seeing that smile banished from his face as, in full view of the staff who adored him, he was led out of the hotel in cuffs, humiliated. *Explain these sick images we found on your computer, Mr. Lewis.* Or, less extreme, getting him drunk enough one night for him to confide in me that he had cheated on Naomi. In the wake of these thoughts, I always felt sick to my stomach, and I know how awful it makes me sound, but you try working every day with the boyfriend of the girl you love and not think unsavory thoughts. In all the time I'd known him, Mark had committed only one transgression—loving Naomi—and he wasn't even aware of it because he had a blind spot when it came to me and my feelings for his girlfriend. If he'd known, he would have been horrified, probably apologetic, because that's just the kind of guy he was. He would have lamented the barrier it created between us, a barrier that already existed, but of which he remained unaware. He would have tried to overcompensate, and that would have annoyed me. He'd have been more discreet, which I would have resented. Or maybe he'd have kicked the shit out of me. Who knows? All I knew for sure was that he wanted us to be friends, probably thought we already were, but that was never going to happen. How could I look at him knowing he got to go home with Naomi every night, got to sleep next to her, and wake up beside her in the morning? I couldn't look at his face without imagining her kissing it, or his hands without seeing him running them over her body. It was bad, and it was unfair, and the only way I could think of to make it better was to concede defeat and remove myself from the equation.

As I crossed through the hazy pool of amber light beneath the dusty chandeliers, the old green shag carpet like kelp beneath my feet, I summoned as much of a smile as I was able. "Hey, man."

He nodded, eyes bright, smile disappearing to accommodate the same look of sympathy I'd seen at the cemetery and would undoubtedly see many more times before the night was through. To his credit, it looked sincere.

"Bummed to hear about your Gran, man. That sucks. You holding up okay?"

"Good as can be expected. Jessop in his office?"

His grin returned. "Yeah, he's in full beast mode today though, bro. Might want to grab a knife from the kitchen before you go wandering into the den."

"Because of the booking?"

"Yeah. He thought we'd be locked up tighter than a bumblebee's asshole about an hour ago. Said there was some movie marathon he was looking forward to watching on AMC or some shit. Had us batten down the hatches and strip the tables. Sent Danny and Leigh home and then suddenly it was all hands on deck and he had to call them back in. He's not a happy camper."

"Is he ever?"

"Guess not, but best to tread carefully today, my friend."

Pete couldn't help using terms of compatriotism like *bro*, *buddy*, *my man*, and *my friend* no more than he could stop calling girls *sweetheart*, and *darling*, and *babe*, no matter how outdated and potentially offensive it was to do the latter. To Pete, the world was his friend until it submitted verified documents to the contrary. As someone who was never good at making friends, or keeping them once I did, that personable optimism was just another thing I envied about him, even if it irritated the shit out of me.

Pete was just a good guy, which is more than I could ever say about myself, and that was just another reason not to like him.

I thanked him and started to move away down the hall.

"Hey," he called after me.

I kept walking but looked back over my shoulder at him.

"Don't let him give you any shit, man. You've had enough to deal with for one day, okay? Even a dick like Jessop needs to respect that."

"Thanks."

He was right, of course. The day had been bad enough, but Jessop was known for a lot of things, and empathy wasn't one of them.

* * *

"I was, of course, sorry to hear about your grandmother," Jessop said.

I stood before his ridiculously oversized mahogany desk—better suited to a lawyer or a banker than the manager of a dying hotel—and attempted a smile. It fell short the longer I was forced to watch him picking at the penny-sized mole on his chin. When it finally dawned on him that the blemish wasn't going to come off, he contented himself with tugging on the fine dark hairs that sprouted from it instead. The whiskey in my stomach started thinking of exits.

"Thanks."

"She was a good woman, I hear."

"She was."

He nodded thoughtfully, as if something profound had passed between us.

"Well," he said, when the only sound in the room was the distant clatter of dinnerware in the kitchen on the other side of his office wall where Danny Sullivan and his wife and sous chef Leigh, were prepping for dinner. "It's probably for the best."

This was not the first time I'd heard someone say that, and while on some level I knew it to be true—she was gone and no longer suffering—the implication still galled me: that the removal of someone from the world could be spoken of as if it were nothing more than a change in the weather. If there was even a shred of doubt about my quitting, I think it fled in that moment as I watched the faux concern pull at the sides of Jessop's mouth. This was a man oblivious to the concerns of others, and to whom this mimicry of condolence was a performance worthy of self-congratulation.

I chose to disregard his pantomime and instead cut right to the heart of the matter. "I'm willing to do a shift tonight, if you need me."

"Yes, Naomi mentioned you might, and I do indeed. We're understaffed as it is and with that idiot Rick out with his ankle—"

"His knee."

"—we'll take all the bodies we can get in here to head off the imminent white storm of snow and octogenarians."

"I also want to hand in my notice. Tonight's my last night."

If Jessop was surprised, he didn't show it, but then, staff turnover in the hospitality industry has forever been exponentially higher than the national average in any given year. Only those for whom options are limited tend to remain. People like Sheri, and Jessop himself. He would be here until someone gave him his marching orders, and even then, I doubted he'd go without a fight. The man was as much a part of the hotel as the old elevator, and like that creaky deathtrap, he'd keep running until the cable snapped and let him fall away into the dark. Some people are so intrinsically linked to their jobs, it's hard to imagine them existing outside of them, like seeing your teacher during summer vacation.

"Is that so?" he said, rolling his massive shoulders and straining the shiny fabric of his suit jacket.

"It is."

Jessop's world seemed a small one. If it extended beyond the hotel, no one here was aware of it. Indeed, it was a topic of frequent speculation, all of it negative. My own theory was less creative than those of my coworkers, who imagined everything from him luring homeless men into his fight club basement to stoking the fires of white supremacy via a secret Facebook group.

I imagined him sitting home alone in front of the TV at night with a glass of whiskey, watching old war movies. Once, in the breakroom, while the staff were naming their all-time favorite movies, Jessop had stopped in the doorway and, in a rare attempt to breach the unbreachable gulf between him and his employees, asked if any of us had ever seen *Sergeant York*. Given the context, we all knew he was referring to a film, but that didn't matter. He was not our friend, and never would be, and given how seldom we had the opportunity to pay him back for treating us like dirt, we couldn't let this one go. In the end, despite the mischievous looks and widening smiles, it was Leigh Sullivan from the kitchen who broke first. "No," she said, "but if you tell me what he looks like, I'll be sure to tell him you're looking for him." That was enough to break the dam of our restraint and by the time we stopped riffing on Leigh's joke, Jessop had moved on to other business.

Afterward I learned that *Sergeant York* was an old war film from the 1940s starring Gary Cooper. Don't ask me why I watched the film. Maybe I wanted to see what it was that Jessop saw in it. If so, I was disappointed. Jessop had never fought in a war for what one must assume were medical reasons, so he was no hero, and too aggressive to sell himself as a pacifist. Which left only a man out of his element surrounded by enemy forces. If that's how he saw himself, and us, then we were right to despise him.

Or maybe it was just a dumb old movie, something to pass the time.

"Well," Jessop muttered. "You're aware we require two weeks' notice."

"I am, but this is my last night."

"Which means we can't take care of you if you quit."

"I do, and I'll be fine."

He sat back. With his dark suit and thinning hair greased back over his narrow skull, he looked like a mortician evaluating the best angle to come at the corpse.

"You've never really cared for me, have you, Mark?"

"I wouldn't say that."

"What would you say, then?"

I exhaled slowly. "I would say your methods in dealing with your staff are..."

"Go on," he said, thin lips twitching in amusement.

"...hostile."

"My managing style is brusque, granted, but that's by design. *Hostile* is a bit of an exaggeration, don't you think? I'm hardly *Herr Commandant*. I prefer the word *firm*."

I shrugged, as uninterested in engaging in a debate about his methods as I was his rehearsed sympathy.

"Remind me: do you have a degree in business management?"

"No."

"No. How many jobs have you had before this one? I seem to recall your resume being rather scant."

"None."

"None. So you wouldn't have much frame of reference, then. Why are you still standing like an attendant at the door? This may be the last chat we ever have. Take a seat."

To humor him, I did, even though it felt like I was being lured into a trap.

"My first job was slaughtering sheep on my uncle's farm in Vermont," he said. "Have you ever been? Beautiful part of the country. Very rural. Very pretty, even though the air smells of shit most of the time. You're a creative fellow, always scribbling your little stories on our napkins, so you're hardly short on imagination. Tell me: can you imagine working twelve-hour days ankle-deep in blood and guts and shit in *June* with flies trying to get into your mouth and a drunken old man screaming abuse at you because you're not moving fast enough for his liking? At age *twelve*, no less!" His eyes were glassy with contaminated nostalgia.

"No, I can't," I told him.

"I did it because I wanted to buy a bike. I was the only kid in my neighborhood who didn't have one. You know what the other kids used their bikes for, other than the usual stuff? A game they called Whip the Sheep. No points for guessing who the sheep was in that scenario. The sheep was a kid who didn't have a bike. They used sticks of bamboo and they whipped me raw, but did I get to cry and whine and complain? Of course not. That would only have encouraged them. Instead, I worked that whole summer in Vermont and bought myself a Schwinn Speedster, and I'll tell you it was the most beautiful thing I ever owned. Neon green, two-tone saddle, cantilever frame, chrome rims. That beauty could slice the wind in half and leave it weeping in the dust."

Behind his glasses, his eyes had gotten misty. The damn bicycle was this guy's Rosebud. It was hard not to connect it to his old green BMW, but maybe that was just coincidence.

"I brought that bicycle on a tour of the neighborhood like an emperor on a new steed and the color of it crept into those bastard kids' eyes, let me tell you. They wanted that bike because it was nicer than theirs, faster than theirs..."

I knew where the story was going before he took it there, because for a man like him, it's the only place a story like that can go. If it hadn't, maybe he'd have been a different person, or maybe his life was just a sequence of ugly jigsaw pieces he spent his time trying to arrange into a nicer picture.

31

"Had it less than forty-eight hours before they stole it. My Pop wouldn't call the cops. Claimed it would embarrass us. Nor did he say anything when pieces of the bike started showing up in our backyard, thrown over the fence from the road. I suppose I could have reassembled it, but by the time the last part materialized, I didn't want that bike, or any other. I just wanted to beat the hell out of those kids."

"And did you?"

Jessop blinked as if I, like one of his poor bicycle parts, had just appeared out of nowhere, dropped into his backyard by some nefarious passerby. For a moment, he looked dazed, still wrapped in the embryo of memory, then he cleared his throat and took a long drag on his cigarette. He exhaled in irritation. "The point I'm trying to make is y—"

"I don't know how easy I have it," I interrupted. "How much harder it was back in your day. The trials you've overcome. The shit you've seen. I had grandparents, and parents, for a while at least. I've heard enough lectures on generational privilege to melt my ears. I get it. I empathize, truly I do, but it's like an astronaut trying to explain space to a mule. Even if it understood, it probably wouldn't give too much of a shit, because this is right now and none of us are going to space."

I hadn't intended to speak so forcefully, but I'd earned the right, and like many a soon-to-be-former employee of a toxic boss, I no longer had reason to hold my tongue or fear retribution. After tonight, I was done, and I was through keeping my thoughts to myself. If Jessop entertained any notions of making my last night difficult, well then, two could play at that game.

Jessop reclined in his chair to a chorus of tortured squeaks. "Know it all, do you? Have it all figured out?"

"I wouldn't say that."

"Satisfy my curiosity then, would you?"

"I should get set up in the bar."

"Sure, in a moment. First, tell me where you're headed once you leave this place."

"I don't know yet."

"Of course you don't. Shall I tell you?"

"I'd rather you didn't."

He stubbed his cigarette out into a clamshell ashtray.

"You're going to go to a big city somewhere. Maybe Portland. Yes, Portland would suit you, I think. A haven for you slovenly intellectual types. You'll get some menial job. Maybe you'll work in another hotel, just until you get the job you actually want, or so you'll tell yourself. You'll also tell yourself you have your drinking under control and that it's always someone else's fault when you get fired or lose a girlfriend. The world will seem increasingly tough, increasingly unfair, and the blame will never be yours."

Done, I rose from my seat. Jessop continued as if I hadn't, his face lit by the freedom of finally being able to share his uncensored opinion of people like me.

"You'll tell yourself there's time, always plenty of time to find your way back to the path that's right and true, to get the job and the girl and the life that you want. You'll even believe it. Until the day you wake up and you're not young anymore and the room around you is as dusty and faded and empty as your dreams."

"You should be writing Hallmark cards," I said, and headed for the door.

"You had a good opportunity here, Mr. Callahan. I gave you that opportunity and you wasted it, as I suspect, you'll waste all others designed to put some character into you. My point was that you take the money and the experience, because any dreams you might have will be ground underfoot by a world that doesn't care a whit about what you want."

"You're one to lecture about character."

The tension between us could have peeled the gaudy red and gold flocked wallpaper off the wall. I would have liked for it to escalate. I wanted it to. It would be somewhere for the maelstrom inside me to go, and I still owed him for the little humiliations I'd been forced to endure under his employ for years.

"I'll be checking the stock in the bar before you leave," he said. "Just to make sure every drop is accounted for. The night's take, too. Despite the enmity between us, I'd hate to have to put a dent in your future by reporting you for theft."

When I looked back at him, his expression was the more familiar one, the one that existed beneath the shabby veneer of professionalism: mistrust, resentment, loathing, though it was not hard to believe that a fair share of that loathing was directed inward.

"There's nothing here I want," I said.

"Oh, I think we both know that's not true."

At his smile, I felt my muscles tense, anger flaring up through my chest. In that moment, I could easily have launched myself across the desk at him, consequences be damned. I'd been through enough over the past few weeks, which left me in the perfect mood to use his face as a punching bag.

"Fuck you," I said instead.

I left before he could respond and slammed the office door shut behind me.

KEALAN PATRICK BURKE

5

NAOMI WAS SITTING AT THE BAR in the Ocean Room, so called because it overlooked the parking lot and the slow, inexorable crawl of the Atlantic beyond, though today it only showed white, as if someone had pulled down the shades. She smiled that debilitating smile at me as I walked in and the sight of her was almost enough to dispel the gloom that clung to my heart at the realization that Jessop had been right. Once I walked out of here, I'd be entering uncharted territory. Life without a plan; travel without a destination. I'd be going against my better judgment and walking blind into a world designed, it seemed, to thwart me. But I was ready to at least try and make my own way. The thrill of not knowing where I might end up and what might happen to me once I got there was only slightly less potent than the all-consuming fear that I was making a terrible mistake.

In a perfect world, Naomi would have been by my side on that trip, cracking jokes in the dark and compensating for my foolishness with her level-headedness. But nothing about the world is perfect. I'd at least lived long enough to learn that much.

I went behind the bar, took a cursory look at the setup. There were two other bartenders in the employ of the hotel. One of them,

Kevin, was reliable. The other, Jackson, was not, and Kevin was out with an injury, which meant Jackson had left the place unwashed and unpolished the night before. "Fuck. I swear Jackson wouldn't wipe his own ass if he could get away with it."

On the other side of the bar, Naomi slid onto a stool. I poured her a coffee.

"So how did it go?" she asked, stirring cream and sugar into the dark brew. The amber track lighting above the bar was good to her, but then, all lighting was.

"Terrific," I told her. "When he wasn't waxing nostalgic about his stolen bicycle, he was warning me not to drink the place dry."

She laughed, a wonderful sound that echoed around a room empty but for us and twenty tables draped in white linen, but I hushed her by flapping my hands. In the Windcrest Hotel, staff laughter was like a klaxon to Jessop, and I needed to be away from him for a while.

I busied myself washing the glasses left behind by the day's small lunch trade.

"What was his beef with you today? You not wearing your tie?"

Until she said, it I hadn't realized I'd forgotten it. It was a small miracle Jessop hadn't pointed it out, given his militaristic rigidity when it came to appearance. I didn't doubt that he'd noticed, but maybe he figured the black herringbone vest and pants would pass even with an open-necked shirt, whereas rolled-up sleeves and a pair of jeans would have given him conniptions. Plus, as short-staffed as he was, he'd hardly have been in a place to argue with me about a tie.

"Shit."

"It wasn't the tie?"

"No. I gave him my notice."

She'd been bringing her cup to her lips. Now she slowly set it back down on the bar. "Your notice? You're leaving? When was this decided?"

"I don't really know. It's been on my mind for a while, I guess."

"And you didn't think to, I don't know, *say* something?"

"Wasn't much point until I was sure I was going to go through with it."

Though it would need to be done at some point, I chose that moment to check the stock in the low fridges because I didn't want to meet her eyes.

"Well that's a kick in the dick." That she sounded genuinely hurt further stirred the waters of my confusion. "Where are you going? And when?"

"I don't know, yet. Going to see what Magda's lawyer says and figure things out from there. Maybe I'll head to Portland." I hated that Jessop had called that one.

"Shit. I want to go. Can I go?"

"Pete would love that."

"I'm sure with time he'll grow to understand." The humorous lilt in her voice told me all I needed to know about how serious she was, so I stayed low and counted the bottles again, even though

39

any idiot could see it was full, not because Jackson had had an uncharacteristic burst of competency, but because business had been slow.

She gave a dramatic sigh. "Can't believe you're leaving. Just like that. This place is going to suck without you. Everything will. And I can't believe you'd just leave me at the mercy of that ogre."

I rose, grabbed a dirty glass, and dunked it in the sink. "Please, if there's anyone here who can handle Jessop, it's you, and maybe Sheri."

Sheri was the only member of the hotel crew who could make Jessop cower. He seldom gave her commands in anything but the sweetest of voices and if she was displeased, he avoided her altogether. This power she had wrought by pretending to lust after him, and while Jessop never responded—at least not publicly—nor did he protest. If anything, he seemed to enjoy her attention. As a result, whenever a member of staff wanted to take an unscheduled day off or leave early, they usually recruited Sheri to soften Jessop up first. I had often wondered what the manager would do if he ever found out she was playing him for a fool. He was not handsome and, at fifty-one, seemed destined to die a bachelor, so it was likely he lived for Sheri's faux adoration.

"One of these days he's going to call her bluff," Naomi said.

"I'd love to be here to see that."

"But you won't be, will you?"

"You have my number, and my email. We'll keep in touch," I said, but again couldn't meet her eyes. We both knew how good distance was for friendships, especially when one side of that friendship would always long for something more.

"Why though?" Naomi said with an exaggerated pout. "Why not just stay if you don't even know where you're going?"

"It's just...it's time. With Magda gone, I don't think I could live in that house by myself."

"So, I'll move in with you. I could use the break in rent. Mr. Foster is gouging me."

"That would never work."

"Why not?"

"Two reasons: Pete, again, who you seem to keep forgetting in your effort to make me stay, and two, you're a slob."

She gasped and threw a sugar packet at me. It smacked against my shoulder and I caught it.

"I just feel like I've already been here too long, and while I hate to say it, I think if Magda hadn't died, I'd never have left. She was the only mother I've known for the longest time. When she got sick, I felt like looking after her was a way of paying her back in some small way. Which annoyed the hell out of her, by the way. She told me I should go and stop wasting my time in this town, but I didn't listen. Not until she was gone, and now I know she was right. The longer I stay, the less likely I am to leave. I need to get out, find out who I am."

"You have a nametag for that."

"You know what I mean."

It took everything in me not to add an addendum about how little I wished to stay just to her best friend and never anything more, that her friendship, as much as I cherished it, came with an equal amount of heartbreak every time I realized she would never love me the same way. "Besides," I told her, "In a few days some other guy'll take over the bar and you'll have a new stud to listen to your woes."

"Are you saying all I do is whine?"

"No. That's not what I meant at all. I just mean places like this have such a big turnaround that it's best not to get too close to anyone. Especially when your boss is someone who seems to enjoy running people out the door."

She shrugged and her hair caught the light. "Well, it's too late. I *am* attached to you, damn it, and I can't believe you're *going*. Just like that. Without even knowing *where!*"

"Okay, fine. Have it your way."

"Yay! You'll stay?"

"No, but you can come with me. We can be like the world's sexiest drifters, sleeping rough, ducking the police, and getting up to all kinds of crazy adventures."

Even in jest, I couldn't believe I'd said something that up until now had been a pleasant albeit impossible fantasy in the back of my mind. But there it was. I'd set myself up for crushing disappointment, but if I hadn't asked, I'd have spent the rest of my life wondering what she might have said if I had. And if by some miracle, she'd agreed, I'd never have given Pete a second thought. I wanted her to be mine and it was a futile pursuit. I knew that, and yet I couldn't let it go. Couldn't let *her* go. I think at that moment I realized how idiotic love makes the most sensible of people. My head knew better; my heart didn't care.

"Or," she said, head cocked thoughtfully. "And hear me out: you *don't* go, and we just leave things as they are. Hell, we can all live together like a bunch of hippies. Start a pot business. Make good use of Magda's garden."

I chuckled, but in my head dangerous words were spilling up over the horizon, words I could and should never say: *I love you, Naomi. I've loved you since I met you and I'm terrified no amount of distance is going to make that go away. Please don't make me go. Please give me a reason to stay. Please rewrite reality so that we fit into it together.*

Even to my own brain, I sounded desperate and pathetic. Worse, as she sipped her coffee and looked at the blank white windows, I knew she'd seen some hint of those words in my face. I cleared my throat and plucked an ashtray from the dirty stack next to the sink.

"It's going to be a hell of a storm," she said. "Just our luck to get trapped with a troupe of seniors for the night. You know they're going to nurse one drink each and be in bed before nine, and we'll have to stick around with nothing to do."

"Speak for yourself. I'm gonna swipe a bottle of whiskey and barricade myself in one of the rooms."

"Now *that's* an idea. I'll bring dessert."

I nodded, but only half heard her. I was looking at her face, at the slope of her cheek, her soft pink lips, and wished, just one time, she would kiss me, to satisfy the curiosity that hit hardest in my dreams.

"Hey Mark," someone said, and I jumped. The ashtray slipped from my hand and plunked into the sudsy water. Naomi flinched and put a palm over her coffee. Foamy flecks of water dotted the back of her hand.

"Sorry," I said and turned to look at Pete who was standing in the doorway with a look of apology on his face.

"Hey babe," he said, grinning.

"Hey sexy," she said back, a knife scoring my insides.

"What's up?" I asked him. *You son of a bitch.*

"How'd it go with The Hunchback?"

"You can probably guess."

"Yeah. Sorry, bro. Guy's a dick."

I shrugged. Another of the reasons I needed to be far from here was that I could be civil enough when alone with Pete, but when the three of us were together and they started trading terms of endearment or worse, getting handsy, it hurt my stomach and brought a hard edge to my voice. Even now, I had to struggle for neutrality. "You need something from the bar?"

He shook his head. "No, man, I wanted to tell you to enjoy the peace while you got it. That tour bus should be here by seven."

Naomi groaned and brought her hands to her face. I looked behind me at the clock over the large mirror behind the bar. It was just after six.

"How many are we expecting?" I asked.

"Eight."

"We should be able to handle that," Naomi said. "Things get too dull, we can pair up and go dancing."

Pete laughed. "Anyway, just thought I'd give you two the heads up. You all set up in here?"

Naomi nodded. "Just about."

"Cool, cool. Hey, if we get stuck here tonight, we should have a party. Get messed up."

"We were just talking about that," Naomi said. "We should totally do it."

He grinned and smacked a hand on the doorframe. "All right, groovy. Talk later, hun. Later, bro."

"Later."

Pete left and I returned my attention to Naomi as she rose from her chair and plucked lint from her uniform. "I'd better go grab a smoke before the guests descend on us. Still can't believe this is your last night. You know we have to give you an epic send-off, right?"

"We'll mess shit up, dude," I said, in an imitation of Pete that was intentionally bad so I could claim ignorance if it caused offense." I had no intention of partying with them. Not now that Pete had invited himself.

With a wink, she left, and I lowered my head, the steam from the water in the sink dampening my face to match my spirits.

6

THE BUS ARRIVED AT SEVEN, just as the worst of the snowstorm lashed the hotel. In retrospect, it's hard not to think that was by design.

I stood at one of the windows looking out over the parking lot, but all I could see was the suggestion of dim yellow lights and some indistinct forms moving slowly from the vehicle to the hotel doors through the white haze.

The wind rattled the glass and the hotel creaked around me like a listing ship. Overhead, the floorboards groaned as ghosts inspected the rooms, but other than the new arrivals, there were no other guests in the hotel. It was the off season and we were remote, and today of all days, nobody had any business being here, ourselves included. Resisting the urge to forensically examine my own true reasons for being here now, I chose instead to wonder why on earth a bus full of elderly people would want to leave the comfort of what I could only assume was their rest home to stay in an otherwise empty hotel in the middle of a winter storm. According to Naomi, they were only booked for the one night. They'd be gone by noon tomorrow, assuming the roads were open by then. There was no conference, no seminar, no shady guy trying to sell them timeshares or reconnect them with their dead loved ones, so what business did they have coming here at all?

Naomi had finished setting up the tables, artificial candles flickering within red glass holders on each one, glasses gleaming, silverware neatly ensconced in their linen wraps. She had gone to confer with the chefs, and I could only imagine how enthused Danny and Leigh were going to be about serving reheated potato and leek soup and Salisbury steak to a handful of cold and irritated customers. It could be argued that they didn't need to be here at all, that Naomi and I could have handled the small group, but I was glad they were. It was one less thing for us to worry about.

Just before seven, as I was heading back to the bar to get the hot water going, predicting a gradual onslaught of hot whiskeys and brandies to warm the old bones of our guests, Jessop appeared in the doorway. My stomach lurched at the thought of a continuance of our tête-à-tête, but quickly forgot about that when I saw the look on his face. To use an old expression, he looked like he'd seen a ghost, or a ghost had seen *him*.

I rounded the bar, my eyes never leaving him, and set about my business while I waited for whatever was coming.

"Callahan," he said, moving to the other side of the bar.

"What's up?"

"The guests are here."

"I know. I saw them pull up."

He nodded, appearing somewhat dazed, his eyes roaming around the bar. "I might need you to...I might need to ask you to do something for me and...you're not going to like it."

Coming from the same guy who'd once asked me to climb up on the roof in the middle of May to clean the sludge from the gutters despite the protests from maintenance and the mutters of liability from Sheri, this was nothing new. The way he was acting, however, was.

"Did something happen?" I asked.

He nodded and finally met my eyes. "I need you to take five and come with me to the lobby."

"Why?"

"There's been an issue with the guests."

"What kind of issue?"

"One of them died on the bus."

* * *

The Ocean Room was separated from the lobby by a long narrow hallway with plush maroon carpeting and intermittent chandeliers sending splinters of amber light across the ceiling and down the flocked wallpaper. There were two doors in the wall to my right. The first was the door to the kitchen, through which I could hear Danny laughing. This was a good sign. When the normally ebullient Englishman was in a bad mood, everyone felt it. Just before the lobby was the door to Jessop's office.

Up ahead, I could see Pete at his desk, talking animatedly to someone I couldn't see. He was using his hands a lot, as Pete always did. I could not see whom he was addressing , but the lobby was alive with low disdainful murmurs.

"I don't get what this has to do with me," I said to Jessop. He too was radiating agitation.

He didn't answer, and when I reached the lobby, I forgot I'd asked.

Snow scattershot the doors. The lights flickered.

A diminutive, pink-faced man with a hat and a sodden navy shirt, his tie and hat askew, was standing before the reception desk, hands on hips, clearly annoyed. He reminded me of Ralph Kramden from *The Honeymooners*, if he'd had a Maine accent and was a foot shorter.

Gathered in the lobby beneath the flickering lights were a crowd of the sickest people I have ever seen in my life, sicker even than Magda at the end. That they were wet, cold, and shivering, only added to the impression that we were hosting, not some bevy of old folks on an ill-timed adventure, but a bedraggled horde of dying refugees. That, or the hotel was being used as a set for a zombie film. Here, a hunched over old man with an ill-fitting suit sucked greedily on an oxygen mask and drummed the fingers of his gnarled free hand against a green tank set on a trolley much like the one I used to ferry beer kegs to and fro. *Clinkety-clink clinkety-clink.* When he inhaled, his chest rattled with phlegm, his cheekbones threatening to cleave right through the yellow parchment-like skin of his face. There, a woman with a walker and cloud-like hair, dressed in a shapeless brown coat with frayed sleeves, jittered in the throes of some nervous disorder, her head occasionally snapping to the ceiling to glare up at the lights with milky eyes. To her right, a Black man in a fedora hat, brown suit, and checkered shirt stood hunched over and leaning on a cane, his mouth hanging open, revealing a pair of slipping dentures. He stared at the bus driver vacantly. Behind him, noticeable as the only one of the party with enough body weight to avert concern, a short doughy man with horn-rimmed glasses and a voluminous tangle of white beard scratched incessantly at a raw red patch of flesh on the side of his face. From clear across the room, I could see motes of skin pluming into the air around his untrimmed nails. He was muttering something to himself, his expression one of unfathomable sadness. It was like looking at an existentialist's interpretation of Santa Claus. Next to him was an old woman with a shock of dyed red hair and a face so deeply wrinkled, it looked more like a map than skin. Eyes so green I could see them clear across the room seemed to peer deep inside my soul like a jeweler studying a gem for flaws. Her eyes were puffy as if she'd recently been crying. Holding onto her elbow was another woman with violet hair and a reed-thin nose, her cheerful expression a direct contrast to that of her friend, but there was no light in her eyes. They were hard as stone. It was evident some trouble existed between these two, perhaps an argument on the bus, or perhaps they just had different ways of coping with the loss of their friend. An old Asian man in sharp suspenders and a vibrant yellow tie doffed his porkpie hat and worried the brim between his fingers as

51

he looked around for the bathroom. Pete pointed down the hall and the old man waved a hand in thanks before shuffling off to relieve himself.

Hair frosted with snow, faces pale like a crowd of the dead, the guests stood watching the exchange my appearance had interrupted, all of them looking desperate for comfort, for warmth...for help.

I turned to Jessop. He breathed like a man who'd just finished running.

"What's going on?" I asked him.

The wind forced a mournful response through the gaps in the main doors and shook them in their frames. Beyond the beveled glass was the bus, similar in size to the old Volkswagens popular among hippies in the 70s. Like the hotel, it had seen better days. Caught in a vortex between the bus and the building, the snow was already working its way up the tires and made it appear to sit unevenly on its chassis. In regal white lettering on a dark blue or black stripe was the word MORNINGSTAR. A vinyl sun shone brilliantly through the hole in the O.

The bus driver looked from Pete to Jessop and me, his eyes red from exhaustion or alcohol, or both.

"I have a dead guy on my bus is what's goin' on," he said. "Who are you?"

"Mark Callahan."

"You a medic?"

"Bartender."

"Great." He sighed. "I'm Buddy Keane."

"It seems a Mr. Atkins fell ill on the journey," Jessop said. "He died before they could get him to a hospital."

"Not much use for a medic then," I said. "Even if I was one."

"Died screamin'," Buddy said with a shake of his head. "Awful thing. Took a few years off my own life to see that, I don't mind tellin' ya."

I looked from Jessop to the driver, confused. "So, the body is *here?*"

"Yup."

"Why?"

"Why what?"

"If you were headed to a hospital, why is the body on the bus and not in the morgue?"

Buddy looked annoyed. "Goddamn road through town was closed. We had to take the backroads to make it here, and those were bad enough." He aimed a stubby finger at the doors and the vehicle parked beyond them. "Take a look at her and tell me you think she'd make it through anythin' bigger than a hailstorm. I love old Suzy to pieces, but I'll be lucky to get her out of the parkin' lot in the mornin'."

It had been a while since I'd had a drink. A throbbing in my temples told me I was going to need one very soon.

"So..." I said.

Jessop looked pained, and to his credit, it appeared genuine. "So, we're going to have to move him."

The driver shrugged. It appeared all etiquette went out the window as soon as his passengers became dead freight. "You have freezers here, don't ya?"

Appalled at the mere suggestion, I looked at Pete, who'd been watching the exchange with grim fascination and no small measure of relief that Buddy's attention was off him. "Pete. You try calling 911?"

"I did. It rings a few times but then I just get static. Probably the storm."

"Try again," Jessop told him. "And if that doesn't work, try the cell under your desk you think I don't know is there."

Pete was too relieved to have something to do other than worry to register that his violation of hotel policy had been exposed.

Buddy gave a curt nod of appreciation. "It's not like I don't feel bad for the guy. I just can't have a stiff on my bus, y'know? The economy being what it is'n all...Word gets around and...well, nobody wants to be driven around in a hearse 'less they've no other choice."

"What happened to him, anyway?" I asked.

"When you drive old folks for a livin', they sometimes end up dyin', though maybe not always like he did."

"What do you mean?"

Buddy removed his cap to reveal a nest of black curls thinning on the crown. Cap in hand, he scratched the bridge of his bulbous nose and sniffed. "I mean he was fine one minute, a shithouse rat the next. Told him stay in his seat but he got up, started yellin' and sobbin' and orderin' me to stop the bus. In the middle of this friggin' weather an' all. Wanted me to let him off, crazy ol' bird. Then, he just went quiet, dropped like a sack of potatoes. His ticker, I'm guessin'. Hit his head pretty good on one of the seats on the way down too, I hear. Eighty-seven years old they tell me and screechin' like an alley cat." He lowered his voice a shade. "Same thing happened to my uncle. Horrible when the mind starts lookin' for the emergency exit."

I glanced at Pete, who shook his head in apology and hung up the phone.

"Okay, look. We at least need to get these people in their rooms so they can dry—"

"Who's with them?" Jessop asked.

"Who's with who?" Buddy asked.

I saw what Jessop meant and wondered why I hadn't before. Then again, when your boss summons you to deal with a dead guy on the same day you buried your grandmother, certain details tend to get overlooked.

"The booking was made by a Mr. Barrows at Morningstar Retirement Community, if I remember correctly," Jessop explained. "And that's what it says on your bus out there, so it's safe to assume that's where they came from?"

Buddy nodded. "Yeah, that's where I picked them up."

"You *picked them up?* They came here unsupervised?"

All three of us inspected the crowd. Given their condition, it should have surprised none of us that one of them hadn't survived the trip here. It would be a miracle if the rest of them survived the

55

trip *back.* Most looked as if the journey from the bed to the bathroom would be treacherous enough and yet here they were, standing in the lobby of a hotel, far from where they belonged. I found myself in agreement with Jessop. It didn't make any sense.

"Where is their caretaker? Their nurse? Their...minder, or whatever you call it?"

"I was told they didn't need supervision." Buddy winced as it dawned on him just how ridiculous that sounded when spoken aloud.

"By whom?" Some of the old Jessop had crept back in, his words laced with impatience and irritation.

"Look guys, I only work there part-time, okay? They call me to ferry this batch of golden oldies from A to Z so I drive the bus—which they own—over there and do the job. I drive a city bus during the week, so I work my tail off for not so much as a thank you. If I forget to ask questions or miss when something's screwy, well, that's on me, I guess, but I don't know what it is you want me to say. Call Morningstar."

"How?" Jessop asked. "The phones are out."

Buddy shrugged. "I'm just doing my job here."

"It didn't seem strange to you that you were bringing a bunch of sick old folks to a hotel during a storm, with nobody to look after them?"

"Look, why you givin' *me* grief? I don't have anythin' to do with where these cronies go or who goes with them. I just drive. That's it, and that's all. Now you got issues with that, you're talkin' to the wrong fella. I'm here." He jerked a thumb back over his shoulder. "So are they. All except the one currently coolin' off in Suzy."

I latched onto this, seeing in his words a chance to keep this already strange situation from turning downright unpleasant, not that I really thought it could be avoided. When a man shows up at your place of business with a corpse in his bus, any semblance of normality has already gone out the window. "Why not pull the bus around back and leave it there until the morning? It's going to be plenty cold out there. Next best thing to a freezer."

Buddy put his cap back on and scoffed. "And what? Lead this parade back onto the bus in the morning for another look at their friend's body? I don't know if you noticed but none of them are in—"

"And I don't think *you* noticed," Jessop said, leaning in close to the driver, "but this is a hotel, Mr. Keane, not a mortuary. If it sounds odd to your ears when I tell you we don't store corpses here, I question the types of establishments you're accustomed to. You're worried about the reputation of a bus whose sole purpose is to drive sick people around whereas *I* am running a hotel, and should it be known that we had a dead person in storage, I guarantee you, *our* reputation wouldn't recover. Don't even get me started on liability and health code violations. And I'm sure his family would love to hear that their dear departed spent the night among slabs of beef and veal. We'd be sued into oblivion."

"Naw," Buddy said. "None of these folks got anyone left to miss them."

57

"I'm willing to overlook the casual cruelty of that remark, but I think you need to hear my words, Mr. Keane. We have never and will never store bodies in my hotel."

I watched Jessop as he spoke. Gone was the shellshocked look I'd seen in the bar. He was alive again, back in his comfort zone: belittling someone lower on the economic ladder, his authority reclaimed. It reminded me why he'd come to me in the first place.

I might need to ask you to do something for me and...you're not going to like it.

A chill rippled through me.

We're going to have to move him.

If Buddy had refused to see reason, Jessop would have asked me, on the day of my grandmother's goddamn funeral, no less, to help carry the old man's corpse into the walk-in freezer. I was sure of it. He wouldn't have been the one sharing the burden either. No. Jessop wasn't one to get his hands dirty when there were underlings to do his bidding. He'd have enlisted Pete to help me.

The thought infused me with the need to beat the smug superiority right off his face, but the shivering crowd in the lobby had seen enough bad things for one night. We would have words later, though, Jessop and I, and maybe I'd blacken his eye before I left this place for good.

"Christ alive," Buddy said, the cap off his head again. He held it by the brim as he wiped a hand over his face. "Fine. I'll pull her 'round back. I don't expect there'll be a problem givin' me a room for the night? Thanks to Mr. Atkins, you've got at least one empty now."

Peach of a guy, I thought.

Jessop, now firmly restored to his original self, made a show of mulling this over, as if there was even the slightest chance he couldn't grant the man's request. At last, he nodded. "We hadn't planned for you, but you're correct. You can take Mr. Atkins' room."

"Great," Buddy said, derisively, as if by dying the old man had somehow infected a room in which he'd never set foot. "Just great." Then he turned to the gathering behind him and his face creased into a smile. Expansively, he said: "Okay, folks. Let's get you all sorted with some nice comfy rooms and a good hot meal."

The crowd shuffled and bumped their way into two small grumbling lines. Wheels squeaked, walkers and canes scuffed against the carpet, joints popped and creaked, but in the end the crowd were still and quiet, but for the drip-dripping of melting snow. No one had opted to investigate the hotel. None of them seemed interested. They just stood and stared in a way that sent a shudder through me.

There was a sudden clank and the grinding screech of unoiled machinery. Jessop winced. "How many bloody times do I have to tell you all not to use that blasted thing?"

His irritation evaporated a second later, however, when the elevator doors scraped open and Sheri Milford emerged, all smiles. "Well, well," she enthused, "our distinguished guests have arrived! How are you, my lovelies?"

This at least seemed to stir the crowd into an approximation of a response. There were subtle nods, the occasional twitch of a smile. Amazing what can happen when you treat people with appropriate respect instead of thinking of them as decrepit cargo. It probably didn't hurt that Sheri was older and had an infirmity of her own, a pronounced limp from when a drunken ex drove their car into a telephone pole and shattered her left leg in six places.

"Sheri," Jessop called. "Would you mind—?"

Already enroute to attending to the guests, Sheri cast a brief look in his direction and the words died in his throat. I envied Sheri that kind of power. We all did. Without saying a word, she had reduced him to silence while still leaving the look open to interpretation. If he dared call her on it, she could claim she was merely giving him affirmation, even though only an idiot would have missed the fire in her eyes that said: *You can see I'm already doing it. Shut the fuck up.*

Unwilling to have his authority so blatantly denied him, Jessop looked at Pete. "Any luck with your cell?"

"None," Pete said.

"That doesn't make any sense," I said. "Cell phones don't need a signal to get through to emergency services."

"Keep trying, Pete." To me, Jessop said: "Callahan, help Sheri get the luggage upstairs. Where the hell is Naomi?"

"In the kitchen, going over the specials."

"Tell her we need her out here to get everyone squared away."

"Sheri and I can handle that."

"Do what I ask, please."

"Do it yourself."

He looked at me, appalled. "What did you say?"

Trembling with barely restrained rage, expression neutral, I leaned in close so only he could hear me. "You were going to have me carry a dead body in here. I've dealt with enough of those today. Push me like that again and it'll be *your* fucking body they'll be carrying out of here, you prick." I didn't wait to see whether he had some pithy response to that. Instead, I made my way over to the guests, where Sheri was playing host better than the man assigned to do it. As I passed Pete's desk, I saw his eyes were wide with admiration and couldn't help but return his smile. "Way to go, dude," he said, quietly.

7

I BROUGHT THE BAGS TO THE DOOR OF EVERY ROOM on the ground floor and then returned to the bar.

Threatening Jessop hadn't made me feel any better. On some level, it felt good to give back to him the kind of disrespect he'd been giving us for years, but it wasn't what I'd wanted. It was impossible to shake the underlying feeling that his demeanor was a façade, a protective screen to keep the world from seeing how alone and afraid and sad he really was. I was mad, sure, but I felt bad for what I'd said to him, no matter how much he might have deserved it.

But that wasn't all. The guests had me rattled too, and I couldn't say why. Maybe it was the storm. Maybe it was the body in the bus. Maybe it was the way they seemed to shift from listless to uncannily aware in the blink of an eye. Or maybe it was a combination of all these things. Whatever foreboding I felt since the bus pulled up, I'd put down to the funereal pall that had clung to me since the moment Magda squeezed my hand and told me she was ready to die, but now I knew it was more than that. It was everything. The presence of the guests here, unaccompanied, at this time of year, was an anomaly. Why had they come? Some of them looked as if they weren't even aware of their surroundings. All of them looked ready to die.

All my gut could tell me was that something wasn't right.

I just didn't know what it was.

* * *

"You said *what?*" Naomi put a hand to her face, tears of delight in her eyes. "Oh God. How did he not fire you on the spot?"

"Why bother? I'll be gone in a few hours anyway."

We were gathered in the bar—me, Naomi, Pete, Sheri, Danny and Leigh—on the pretext of a staff meeting should Jessop storm in on us as retribution for my insolence. Really the rest of them had gathered as the word passed from one staff member to the next about what I'd said to him in the lobby. I admit their admiration helped ease the guilt a little.

"Can't believe the wanker wanted to stash a bloody corpse in my fridge," Danny said, appalled. "If he'd tried that shit, it wouldn't just be *your* last night, Mark, believe you me."

"Aw, big tough man," Leigh cooed, flicking his earlobe with her nail. He flinched away from her but couldn't repress the smile.

Danny was British, his wife American. Apparently, theirs had been a green-card marriage that had accidentally and quite wonderfully blossomed into something more. They had two kids now—who, thanks to the demands of the job, saw more of Leigh's parents than their own—and planned to open their own *Euro-*

American bistro in Bar Harbor as soon as they could afford the risk. It was hard not to think of them as made for each other, though they couldn't have been more different in appearance. Danny was five-foot five, built like a small tank, and covered in scars, piercings, and tattoos. He was an excellent cook but had learned by apprenticing under better chefs and had no formal education in that regard.

By contrast, Leigh was tall, lithe, and well-spoken. She had trained at the New England Culinary Institute, after which she'd worked everything from front-of-house to sous chef at an impressive number of prestigious eateries. Personally and professionally, she had a grace her husband lacked, but together they made for an intriguing and amusing pair. A closer look, however, revealed they were not so different after all, for while Leigh had no *visible* tattoos, she did have a crimson butterfly on her back and a black ankh on her right wrist, and her jet-black hair was threaded with pink.

"What I can't figure out is why he was willing to go along with it in the first place," I said, automatically wiping down the bar though it didn't need it. All the staff but Leigh were drinking. Sheri reckoned the sous chef might be pregnant again, but nobody knew where they'd have found the time. "I mean, he seemed shook when he came in here. When have we ever seen him like that other than that time the owners told him the menu was shit?"

"To be fair," Danny said, "they weren't wrong. He cribbed it from some fussy hotel restaurant in New York and thought it would fly out here in the sticks where people want a good clam chowder, not truffled fuckin' eggs."

"I still can't believe you said that to him," Naomi said.

"Not like he didn't have it coming." I told her.

Pete had been silent. Now he shook his head and put his arm around Naomi. I had to struggle not to avert my gaze. "I should have called off. Those old folks give me the creeps."

"Typical millennial," Leigh said with a smirk, and with a toothpick, stirred the ice in her glass of water. But Leigh and her husband hadn't seen the guests. I wasn't even sure Naomi had. Those who had seen them seemed in tacit agreement with Pete's appraisal. In truth, I was glad to hear him say it aloud.

Sheri rolled her eyes. "You know, I'm no spring chicken myself, but it will never cease to amaze me the way you young people treat the elderly. You do realize they didn't just appear on earth as old people, right? You do realize they were once you: young people with hopes and dreams and goals of their own. They worked long hours and lived through shitty times and sacrificed God only knows what to provide for their children. The old get old because they pulled off a miracle and didn't let life kill them. That takes strength, persistence, commitment, and you should respect that. They're not a bunch of husks walking around with nothing inside them. They're people, and that's how you should treat them."

"Yeah," Danny said with a smirk as he pushed away from the bar. "You should listen to her. She'd know, bein' as how she's older than the pyramids." He hurried away, ducking as a damp washcloth came sailing toward his head. He was lucky it hadn't been a glass.

"Keep running, spud-boy," Sheri said. "You'll remember what I said when your kids are sticking you in some godawful rest home to die."

"I'll never be too old to give them a good what-for," he said.

Leigh rose from her seat and shoved her glass toward me. "He thinks he'll live forever," she said by way of apology and followed her still-laughing husband to the kitchen.

Sheri shook her head. "It's easy to be arrogant when you think you're immortal," she said. "Take it from me: time passes quickly, and the golden years aren't long coming."

"Well, you still look great to me," Pete said, and Sheri leaned over on her stool to give him a peck on the cheek. "You're full of shit, Petey, but I love you. And now, ladies and gentlemen, if you'll excuse me—" She drained her gin and tonic and belched lightly before handing me the glass. "—I must attend to our distinguished guests." And then she was gone, leaving me, Naomi and Pete at the bar.

"You know Mark's leaving?" Naomi asked him as a fresh gust of wind huffed against the windows and sighed mournfully through the gaps in our crumbling fortress. It was already full dark out there, the snow like shredded daylight.

Pete was shocked. "What? Why? You can't leave, dude. This place will suck balls without you."

"It sucks balls now, Pete."

67

"That's true, but still. Shit, man." He looked genuinely aggrieved, and for the second time that night, I felt bad for ever wishing him ill.

"I'll check in from time to time."

"No he won't," Naomi said sourly.

"No you won't," Pete agreed. "Maybe we can come see you though. Where you going?"

"Not sure yet. Portland, maybe."

"Ah, Portland is a blast. Been there a buncha times. Great club scene."

Naomi socked him in the shoulder. "Don't encourage him, dildo."

"Ow! What?"

"We can't let him get away that easy."

He raised his hands and winced. "Okay, sorry, sorry."

My smile was genuine as I watched their banter, but it faltered a little under the weight of a sudden unexpected realization: I had always thought of Naomi as the girl I'd never have and Pete the obstacle keeping her from me, even though I was not naïve enough to think there wasn't more to it than that. But when it came down to it, these two were, above all else, my *friends.* Somehow, perhaps because of my feelings for Naomi, I had never seen them that way. And I should have. If I had, I could have enjoyed them for the good people they were.

So, stay.

Perhaps if the realization had come sooner, I'd have canceled my plans, rough as they were, but I couldn't change them now. It was too late. My engine had stalled, maybe as far back as the day Magda took me in, and I'd been idling ever since. Though it would kill me to be away from Naomi, it would kill me even more to stay and watch her life go on with Pete or whomever else ultimately took his place who wasn't me. I needed to establish myself somewhere else, become someone not governed solely by my own confused emotions. I needed to put down roots of my own.

"I should get back," Pete said, stooping to give Naomi a quick kiss on the lips.

Again, that pulse of hurt.

"And you," he said, pointing a finger at me. "This isn't over, *mi hermano*. Not by a long shot."

I raised my hands in surrender. "Whatever you say, boss."

"Damn right I'm the boss."

Naomi and I watched him leave, and then she reached across the bar and grabbed my hand. Her eyes were wet. I could have drowned in them.

"I'll give you ten thousand dollars if you stay," she said.

"You don't have ten thousand dollars."

"Okay. Fifty dollars." She laughed. "Shit. I don't want you to go. Don't go. And I'm not crying, just so you know. My contacts itch, that's all. Why are you going?"

My heart almost exploded as a tsunami of explanations rushed into my mouth, every single one of them true. Panic fluttered in my chest.

I have to get a life.

I have to grow up.

69

I can't be in this town with its memories of death.

I'm lost.

I love you.

I—

"Because of you," I said, and the resultant silence was so profound, I could have sworn even the storm stopped heckling the hotel.

Naomi sat back in her chair and slowly relinquished her hold on my hand. I saw no anger in her face, no hurt...only confusion. *What did you say?* Then it dawned on me that there were any number of ways my words could have been interpreted, and if she chose the wrong one, she might deduce something else entirely. But then, all of it was wrong in some way.

"What I mean is..." I started to say, but her look drained me of the power to finish.

"What are you saying to me right now?"

Then the wind spoke to me, or at least that's what it sounded like at first. I followed it to the door where The Man with the Cane was leaning into the room, one spindly arm forcing the door open so he could see me. I had forgotten to open them.

"Are you open for business?" he inquired again, and I nodded dumbly at him, and then looked at Naomi, but she was already off her stool and headed to attend to him.

Thus began the longest night of my life.

8

I HAD ALWAYS PREFERRED A PACKED BAR to an empty one. Time flies when you can't stop to watch it, or to think. I was glad when the guests began to slowly find their way into The Ocean Room.

It was a veritable parade of illness and blue hair; oxygen masks and rouge; creaking bones and hair cream; liver spots and yellowing dentures; stiff joints and frayed cuffs, all meandering into the room as if it was a welcome rest stop at the end of an arduous journey. Which, by all accounts, it had been. Buddy might have been blasé about losing a passenger, but these people had known Atkins, and while the debate about what to do with his remains had been in full swing, nobody, myself included, had stopped to consider how they were handling it.

I watched them squint at the maritime-themed paintings on the wall, the stuffed marlin nailed above the bar, the bottled ships on the lintel, the gleam of glass, the glow of the lights, the shudder of the windows behind the long red curtains I had pulled across them. They consulted each other about the décor, some unimpressed, most approving, others indifferent to anything but the seats. Walkers chafed the soft wine-colored carpet as bodies eased into chairs and sighs were drowned out by the storm. The scents of lavender, primrose and talcum powder filled the air.

Last to enter was the old woman with the shock of red hair, her face pinched and waxy looking in the ambient light. She passed the bar and, ignoring the summons of her fellow guests, sat by herself at one of the many unoccupied tables. I watched her fish some tissues from her purse and wondered if I should attend to her, but then figured I'd be summoned if assistance was required. Besides, and I hate to admit it, I planned to avoid any more drama for the rest of this night. Confessing to Naomi had been one step further than I'd ever planned to go, and no amount of whiskey could calm the nerves thrumming in my stomach, though I kept trying. As a result, the room moved a fraction of a second too slow, the wind seemed to have invaded my head, and the murmuring crowd sounded as if they were behind the bar with me, needling and insistent.

I brewed some coffee, spilling half the measure onto the floor my hands were shaking so bad.

A shadow, lithe and oily, yawned across the length of the room, dimming the lights, and making rusty blood of the walls.

Drunk. Drunk and frightened. Of what, I didn't know. Of the feeling in the air, maybe, the spasming of those shadows that seemed to be standing an inch away from where they belonged. Or maybe I was unsettled by the look of dread expectation in the faces of the guests. The look of imminent *something*.

Naomi was busy. I told myself that's why she only came to the bar for drink orders and left without a word once they were fulfilled, but I'd seen her less flustered with three times the crowd and any idiot could tell she was trying to avoid conversation, and who could blame her? I'd dropped a bomb from which we might never recover.

It was, I suppose, typical of me.

I reached into the small refrigerator beneath the register, searched for milk and found none. With a mumbled curse, I grabbed the coffee pot and sloshed the black brew into the cup, then drank deeply until it felt as if someone with a rusty knife had pared the skin from the roof of my mouth. The sensation was excruciating, and I winced into the palm of my hand. But it was pain, searing and real and almost enough to bring me back to myself. Cup in hand, I rose just in time to see the red-haired woman turning away from the bar, where she'd been waiting for some indeterminate amount of time.

"Oh, I'm sorry Ma'am," I said, every word feeling as if spoken around a red-hot coal. "I didn't see you there."

She turned back, the grief on her face a shocking reminder that I had not yet given myself time to properly mourn my own loss.

"I was sorry to hear about your friend," I said.

"Please," she said, eyes shimmering. "Please." She looked very small and brittle, her head lowered, shoulders hunched as if trying to shield herself from the people in the room behind her. Like she feared attack.

73

"Can I get you something? Would you like to sit down?"

"I'm," she said, her lower lip trembling. "I'm so terribly sorry."

Momentary confusion led me to believe she knew about Magda, but how would she have come by that information?

"You have nothing to be sorry for. Let me get you a drink. What would you like?"

She turned to look behind her and her necklace caught the light. At the end of a long chain was an amulet depicting a leafless tree with sprawling limbs and chaotic roots trapped inside a gold circle.

"Ma'am?"

I set the coffee down and leaned over the bar, so that our faces were almost touching. Her hands were gnarled, the knuckles red and swollen in contrast to her thin white fingers.

"What's the matter?" I asked, sliding a hand over hers, and had to resist pulling away just as quickly. Her skin was ice cold.

When she didn't answer, I followed her gaze to her companions. Their faces were smeared with shadow, the windows still rattling as the snow hissed against the glass, the sound muted only slightly by the thick curtains. Naomi moved among them like a creature of light, making cheerful inquiries, checking to ensure they were being looked after, seemingly oblivious to the gold sparks I saw in their eyes.

I filled a tall glass with water, drank it, dumped it in the sink and repeated the process with another glass. This one I filled with ice and placed it in front of the old woman. "Here," I said. "Drink this."

When she looked back at me, tears were streaming down her face. "I didn't know this is what it was," she said. "I didn't know it would be like this at all. If I...if I had, please believe I'd never have come. I'm so sorry. So sorry."

She hoisted her purse up from the chair next to her and rummaged around inside it. Spent tissues and a tube of lip balm tumbled out onto the bar. A quarter tinged off the gold rail and disappeared. She ignored it and withdrew a crumpled twenty-dollar bill, which she slid across the surface of the bar. I offered her a reassuring smile.

"Can I get you a drink?" I asked as she blew her nose into one of the sodden hankies.

"I'm so sorry for what they're going to do to you," she finished, and with a frightened look toward the door, hurried away from me.

"Big ass bourbon, no ice, no nothin'," a familiar voice said.

Buddy Keane sat down on the seat where Naomi had been less than an hour earlier and let out a long low breath. "Man, it's been a day. My dogs are barkin. What was wrong with Dorothy? She looked upset."

Dorothy had returned to her seat, but now there were others sitting with her, their hands emerging from the shadows of their sleeves like pale crabs to scuttle their comfort over her.

I sighed. "She lost her friend today, remember? I think it's been a rough day for everyone."

75

"I didn't realize they were that close." He noticed the twenty-dollar bill on the bar before him. "Hey, least she left you a decent tip. That's a surprise. No offense to the old folk, but they tend to be a little tight with their pensions."

I fetched his bourbon for him.

"Thanks."

I was still unsettled by the encounter with the old woman. To anyone else, what was happening at her table might have looked like friends consoling one of their own. I don't know why but it didn't look like that to me. In a million years, I couldn't point out any one thing that gave the impression of intimidation, a ridiculous notion among people so frail, and yet it was there in the way they leaned in so close to her, in the set of their mouths. And the queer light I thought I'd seen in their eyes.

I'm sorry for what they're going to do to you.

"Hey, you there?" Buddy asked, waving a hand in my face.

"Sorry. What did you say?"

He indicated the folded over note on the bar.

"Twenty clams just for a glass a water she didn't even drink. She must've taken a shine to you, my friend. Might be you've got yourself a date for the evenin'."

I stared at the note. "Yeah. I should give it back to her."

"Don't bother," he said with a shrug. "Knowing Dorothy, she's already forgotten she even met you. Mind like a leaky faucet, that one."

"What's the matter with her?"

"Same thing that's the matter with the rest of 'em, I suppose. They're old. On their last legs an' all that. Me, I'd rather be nice and soused when my time comes, so if you wouldn't mind..." He drained his glass and held it out for a refill.

I slid the note from the bar and tossed it next to the till, my intent to return it when I got the chance.

When I delivered his drink, there were another two customers at the bar, the doughy man with the beard and The Man with the Cane. I hadn't heard their approach and their smiles did nothing to stave off the chill. It looked rehearsed. I noticed too that they were wearing the same spindly-tree amulets I'd seen around Dorothy's neck. After I served them, and they were out of earshot, I asked Buddy what they were.

"Some church thing."

"Like a religion?"

"Yeah. Same symbol that's on the chapel door in the rest home. I see it every time I go in there to take a leak. Don't know much else about it, to be honest. I'm Catholic myself, though not a very good one. Too drawn to sins of the flesh, if you know what I mean."

I did, but had no desire to have them detailed for me—his lecherous expression was bad enough—so I steered the conversation back on track.

"Must be a pretty exclusive religion."

"You know how it is these days. New ones pop up all the time. All it takes is for some loon with a bit of money and charm and suddenly the FBI are surrounding your ranch. World's gone nuts.

But, way I figure it, if it gives 'em some kind of peace and they're not causin' anyone any harm or knocking on doors tryin' to convert us all, they can have any religion they like."

Naomi appeared next to him and huffed a strand of hair out of her eye and slid an empty water jug atop the bar. "Can you fill this with ice for me please?"

"Sure."

I did and with a muttered thanks, she was gone.

"Oof," Buddy said, just as I knew he was going to. "She don't look short on ice, that one."

The night began to move.

I got the distraction I'd hoped for and took a break wherever available to refresh my coffee.

An hour later I was tired, but less disorientated and my disposition had improved greatly. Buddy retired for the night, so I struck up short conversations with some of the guests and started to question my initial impression of the group. For the most part, they seemed a pleasant crowd, but further scrutiny revealed that all of them seemed to be suffering one terminal malady or another. They weren't just sick; they were dying. The Ocean Room was like the world's most ambient sick ward. It made me wonder if perhaps this little pilgrimage had been such a bad thing after all. Though they didn't seem fit to be traveling, why should they be denied a short trip if it freed them from the familiar gloom of their surroundings for a while?

I recalled Magda at the end, lying in her bed at home where she'd insisted she be allowed to die, and not in some soulless white room that smelled of disinfectant and other people's cancer. After telling me she didn't have long, Doctor Bradford waited in the hall. He'd asked me to ask again if she wanted a priest. I told him she was an atheist. He almost succeeded in keeping the judgment from his eyes.

"You'd be surprised how often they convert once the fear of meeting God as a stranger settles in on them," he'd said in a way he probably thought was patrician but came across as pious. I left him and God in the hall and went to say goodbye. It took much longer than he'd predicted, and she slept through a great deal of it. At the end, as the shades came down on my grandmother's life, she neither accepted nor rejected God. She simply smiled up at me and said: "I'm ready now, Mark. Please look after yourself, and remember, life is everything. Love is too." Then she tilted her head back a little, closed her eyes, and exhaled. There was nothing dramatic about her passing. She had simply been alive one moment and dead the next. It was me who was left with the regret that we hadn't lived more while she was able and that I hadn't loved her enough.

The storm rattled the building in its skin with greater force than before. The guests had their dessert, apple pie and ice cream for some, bowls of Jello for the rest. By now, Danny and Leigh would be cleaning up. In one corner, a low singing started. It wasn't a song I recognized and after a while, the single voice became a chorus.

Buddy left, and his meager tip reminded me of Dorothy's money, but when I grabbed the bill from its place by the till and unfolded it, I stopped dead, the note curling open like a dying fish in my palm.

Dorothy had written two words in orange lipstick across Andrew Jackson's face.

GET AWAY.

9

ON'T IT BE GOOD TO GET OUT OF this horrid old suit, Dottie?" the lady with the violet hair said as I approached Dorothy's table. The rest of the guests had moved away and gathered in the gloom to enjoy their post-dessert coffee. Some were still singing that strange song, which put me in mind of long-forgotten gospel songs played at varying speeds on an old gramophone. It made my head hurt the harder I tried to divine the words.

"Ma'am?" I said, when I reached them. Dorothy was sitting with her head lowered, lips downturned, still looking small, as if she wanted to crawl inside herself to escape. Her hands were clenched in an unsuccessful attempt to keep them from trembling. Next to her sat the woman with the violet hair and hard eyes. She sat sideways in her chair and leaned in close to her sobbing friend, one arm hooked across the back of Dorothy's chair. So intent was she on the upset woman, it took her a moment to notice me standing there. When she did, her smile stopped short of her eyes.

"We're fine, thank you."

I ignored her and to Dorothy said: "Ma'am, is everything all right?"

"I told you, we're fine. We have everything we need."

"If it's all the same, I think I'd rather hear it from Dorothy."

Dorothy wouldn't look at me.

"Are you sick? Do you need assistance?"

Still nothing. She just looked down at her hands and sniffled softly.

I looked at the woman. "I'd keep a close eye on her if I were you. She's not looking well."

She chuckled dryly. "I think if you'll take a look around, you'll see that none of us are."

"Still. She's very upset. Might not hurt to keep tabs on her."

"Which is what I was doing before you poked your nose in. Why do *you* care anyway? Shouldn't you be behind the bar sneaking whiskeys or throwing lusty eyes at that pretty young waitress? What was her name? Naomi?"

"That's none of your business."

"My name is Agnes, by the way, and you're Mark, isn't that right?"

I was about to ask how she knew when I remembered the gold nametag on my waistcoat.

"It's good that we've been introduced," Agnes said. "I have a feeling one day we're going to be very close, and I for one cannot wait."

"Look, I'm just asking if she's all right."

"She's probably not." Agnes reached into her purse and withdrew a pack of Menthol cigarettes. "But she will be before the night is through. And trust me, honeybear, after spending most of my life working in theater, I can spot melodrama a mile away." She pronounced it *theatah.* "What poor Dotty doesn't understand is that to truly *sell* a scene, you must commit to it *entirely,* body and soul. Otherwise, what is it other than a charade?"

"There's no smoking in here."

"Would you prefer I go outside and die of cold? I'm sure your manager would love that. You two seem so close." She looked up, glassy eyed, the cigarette poised in front of her lips. "Just imagine the headlines: 'Two Pensioners Die at the Windcrest Hotel!'" She smirked, thumbed her lighter and lit up.

Her smug demeanor rolled with the smoke over the table and rose like fog into my face. My knuckles tightened. The brief respite from anxiety had evaporated at the sight of Dorothy's note. This little confrontation hadn't helped. I'd worked in this bar for years and had had my share of difficult customers, but the mirthful threat I saw in this woman's eyes was new and confusing to me. It was not arrogance, haughtiness, superiority. It was the smug look of dark confidence only present in the eyes of those who intend to do you harm.

Deciding it wasn't worth it, I shook my head and was about to turn away when a hand shot out and latched onto my wrist. The grip was tight and painful. I looked at Dorothy, who shuddered and stared at a point somewhere to the right of my face. I tried to tell myself it was just the light from the tabletop candles I was seeing reflected in her pupils.

"Go home," she said.

"Perhaps we should have him join us for a drink instead." Agnes reached across the table toward Dorothy, twirled her fingers around a strand of the woman's red hair and tugged once, hard enough to elicit a wince and jerk Dorothy back toward her.

"We have everything under control here," Agnes said. "Don't we, Dotty?"

She leaned closer until I thought she was going to kiss Dorothy on the cheek. Instead, she smiled, opened her mouth, and with a tongue that was inexplicably black, as if she'd been sucking on licorice, licked the side of the old woman's face from the corner of her mouth to her eyelid.

They were mad, both of them. Call it dementia, delusion, the kind of craziness that comes before death, I didn't know and didn't care. I couldn't take what I was seeing, not after being so close it to it for the past few weeks, months, however fucking long it had been since Magda got sick.

"You know where to find me if you need anything," I mumbled and headed back to my post.

"Indeed we do, honeybear," Agnes called after me. "And indeed we will."

For the next half hour, I tried in vain to keep my eyes off that table. Eventually, Dorothy stopped weeping and fell silent, her gaze fixed on something directly in front of her, though all I could see was an old oil painting of the *Lusitania* on the far wall.

I tried to shake the image of Agnes licking Dorothy's face, but it wouldn't leave me. I poured myself another glass of whiskey and drank it hunkered below the counter. Not that there was much point in hiding anymore. Apparently, everyone knew what I was doing.

When I rose, the whiskey searing my throat, Naomi was standing before me. She looked worried.

"Hey," I said, startled.

"We need to talk."

"I know we do. Listen, I'm sorry about what I said earlier."

"Not about that."

"What, then?"

"Have you seen Sheri?"

"Not for a while. Why?"

The guests were watching us with that strange low light in their eyes, and I felt a chill pass through me.

No one was singing now.

"I can't find her," Naomi said. "Nobody can."

"When did you see her last?" I poured her a tonic and spiked it with a splash of vodka.

"Reception. I was talking to Pete."

About me? I wondered. I know there were bigger concerns at that moment, but I couldn't help but worry. Had she told him what I'd said? And if he took it as well as she had, should I add a dustup with him to the ever-growing list of bad things in store for me? I couldn't envision it, but it was turning out to be a night of firsts.

"She came back from helping the woman with the walker to her room, and she looked sick. Like, real sick." She took a long draw of her drink and nodded her thanks for the Smirnoff enhancement. Tucking her hair behind her ear, she glanced over her shoulder at the guests, noted their attention, and then turned back to me, voice lowered. "I asked her if she was okay, and she looked at me like she didn't even know me. She was holding her throat."

"Where did she go?"

"She wasn't responding to us, so I ran to get Jessop, but his office door was locked. He was in there though. The light was on, and I could hear him moving around. Probably jerking off."

"I could have gone the rest of my life without that visual, thanks."

"You know me, right? I don't freak out over anything."

Well, almost anything, I thought, remembering the look on her face when I confessed that she was my reason for leaving. "I know."

"But it looked like she'd been attacked. I can't be sure because it's pretty hard to see anything under those shitty lights in the lobby, but I thought there were tiny scratches on her face and neck."

I rubbed a hand over my face. "We need to find her."

"You believe me, right?"

"Of course I do."

"Thank Christ, because there's something else." She took another quick glance over her shoulder. "Two things, actually. The first is that she was wearing one of those things around her neck that all of *them* are wearing."

"The tree thing?"

"Yeah."

"She probably found it on the floor somewhere and wore it until she could return it. What else?" I knew even as I said it that Sheri wasn't the type to wear someone else's jewelry while she looked for its owner.

"It was Pete who noticed it, so I can't say for sure if this is true, but I don't know why he'd say it if it wasn't..."

The track lighting above our heads dimmed for a moment. I shivered, feeling as if something had moved between us.

"He said she wasn't limping anymore."

I fixed myself a shot, no longer caring who saw it. The night had come unmoored since the arrival of our guests and I needed to fortify myself for whatever was coming next. "You didn't see where she went after that?"

"When I got back to reception, Pete said he grabbed his cell to try 911 again and when he looked up, she was gone."

"When was this?"

"About twenty minutes ago, though it feels like an hour."

"You check anywhere else?"

"No, I couldn't. I had to get back here."

"You mind watching the bar for me for a little while? I won't be long. "

Naomi nodded and seemed to sag against the bar.

"Hey," I said.

She looked at me.

"It's going to be all right. In a few hours, all of us will be drinking and laughing about this, okay?"

"Okay." She sounded like she didn't believe it.

I couldn't blame her. I didn't believe it either, especially considering something that had occurred to me when we were talking to Buddy Keane in the lobby about Atkins. When Jessop instructed Pete to use his cell phone to call 911, Pete said he couldn't get a signal, and Naomi told me he tried again when Sheri appeared injured. So either Pete was lying to us, which was highly unlikely, or something other than the storm was interfering with the signal.

As I walked out of the bar, I took out my own cell and dialed 911.

Despite being almost fully charged, the phone died in my hand.

* * *

To be thorough, I checked the kitchen again and found Danny and Leigh idling, the line already sparkling clean, the floors swept, and everything put away. They were sitting side by side on one of the prep tables under the harsh glow of the fluorescents, engaged in a lively debate about canned tomatoes as a viable substitute for fresh in certain dishes, specifically chicken curry. Leigh advocated the use of the former, which Danny thought anathema. When they saw me, she jumped down and hurried to the fridge.

"I made pumpkin bars. You get to the be the first to tell me they're wonderful because Jerkenstein here doesn't eat pumpkin."

"Gives me the trots," he grumbled.

"Thanks Leigh," I told her. But I'm not real hungry right now." This was a lie. I couldn't remember when I'd last eaten, but now was the not the time to think about food. Anything she served me would only have reeked of death or brought the whiskey up into my throat. "Save it for me for later," I said, to avoid appearing ungrateful.

She flashed jazz hands at me. "Drizzled with caramel sauce..."

"Sounds delicious, but listen, has Sheri been through here?"

Danny shook his head. "Sorry, mate. Nobody has, except Naomi. Even Jessop kept his arse away tonight. What's up?"

"She looked sick, and now we can't find her. We're getting a bit worried, to be honest."

"Well, we'll keep an eye out for her," Danny said.

Scowling, Leigh slapped him in the back of his bald head. He looked at her questioningly, then, reading the obvious command in her face, sighed, undid his apron, and tossed it on the table.

"Right, yeah. What I mean is, Mark, my son, let's go find this errant bird of ours."

KEALAN PATRICK BURKE

10

THE LIGHTS FLICKERED WHEN WE STEPPED out into the hall. We both looked up at them. I tried not to attribute malevolent intent to the shadows that sprouted from the walls and rose from the floor, but the distant moan of the wind did nothing to dispel the sense that the hotel itself came alive whenever the light died.

"Hope to fuck William thought to gas the generator," Danny said, referring to the maintenance man, whose presence had been deemed unnecessary given the size of the booking. In retrospect, it had probably been foolish to send away the only guy who could ensure everything kept working during a violent snowstorm. "All right. How do you want to do this?"

"I guess we should split up. I'll check outside where she goes to smoke, then the break room and the rooms on the ground floor, bathrooms included. You want to take the upper floors?"

"Sounds like a plan. Sheri's got access to all the rooms, doesn't she?"

"She has the housekeeping key."

"How'll we know she didn't just let herself into one of the vacant ones and grab some kip? Makes sense she might want to crash if she was feelin' poorly. It's what I'd do."

"Without telling anyone? I don't know. It doesn't sound like her. I guess just knock on some doors. Most of the guests are still in the bar so you don't have to worry about disturbing anyone. If she did just take a nap in one of the vacant rooms, she's unlikely to have locked it behind her, so try them all."

"Gotcha."

"Meet you back at reception in say, thirty minutes? I don't want to leave Naomi alone in the bar any longer than that."

"Why? She okay?"

"She's a bit rattled. It's the guests I'm not comfortable with."

"Those old fogies? They seem all right."

It would have taken too long to explain and if I tried, Danny was likely to think me crazy. "They're just an odd bunch," I said, and that seemed to satisfy him. Together we walked the hall toward reception, where Pete was staring dumbly out through the glass doors. When we reached Jessop's office, I told him to go on ahead.

"See you soon," he said.

"Right, and hey, Danny?"

He raised his eyebrows at me.

"Be careful."

"Of what?"

"Just...be careful."

He looked confused by that but didn't question it any further. I pictured Naomi back in the bar, how it would feel if *she* went missing. I didn't like the thought of her there by herself, or of Leigh alone in the kitchen, so I resolved to make my search a quick one.

* * *

It was time to bring Jessop up to speed.

I hammered a fist on his door. Waited.

Something shuffled inside the office. Naomi was right. Jessop was in there. And just like when she'd tried to summon him, he didn't answer.

"Open up," I said, then employed the only tactic I knew was sure to get his attention. "Sheri's missing."

It worked. A few moments later, the lock clicked, but he didn't open the door. I let myself in.

Jessop was sitting behind his desk, nursing a glass of bourbon, and smoking a cigar. His hair was in disarray and there were bags under his eyes. He looked like he'd aged ten years in the few hours since I'd last seen him.

"Thought we weren't allowed to smoke inside the hotel," I said.

"You're not. I do as I please."

"Okay Henry the Sixth. What do you want to do about Sheri?"

"She'll turn up," he said. Framed on the wall over his shoulder was a certificate from some business school in Syracuse, NY. It might as well have been on the moon for all I knew of it.

"That's it? She'll *turn up?*"

He clasped his hands on the desk and looked evenly up at me. It was hard to tell what he was thinking, but I admit I was taken aback by his ambivalent response to the news that a woman for whom he clearly felt a great deal of affection was nowhere to be found.

"What would you like me to say, Callahan? That she's in trouble and we should organize a mass search? Turn the hotel upside-down?"

"It'd be a better start than *she'll turn up*, sure."

"Why should I?"

He wasn't done. There was an odd look in his eyes I wasn't sure I'd ever seen before.

"You think I don't know she gets paid for hours she's not even here? That she cheats the system because she knows I'll never call her on it? That she feels pity for me and acts like she cares because she doesn't have the heart to tell me she finds me loathsome? Or that I haven't heard her talking about me in ways that would make a weaker man want to never show his face in public again? Yes, Callahan, I do believe she'll turn up because half the time she isn't where she's being paid to be or doing what she was hired to do, and if she doesn't miraculously appear with some ridiculous excuse, if she's *not* outside smoking or in the bathroom yucking it up with Naomi or Leigh, or on the phone to her latest lover in a long line of them, and some grave misfortune *has* befallen her, well then, I suppose, like poor old Mr. Atkins, that's just bad luck. There's a lot of that going around of late."

Without waiting for him to tell me I could, I sat down in the seat opposite him. His eyes followed me with the wariness of a dog unsure whether it's going to be forgiven or further abused. Something was wrong, something he wasn't telling me, because the things he had spontaneously decided to share with me today were not typical of him. First a childhood tale of bullying and now a confession that he'd known all along that Sheri had been playing him for a fool? It didn't add up.

"What happened?" I asked him. "What's the matter with you?"

"Nothing."

"Bullshit. You're not yourself."

"I've been given the opportunity to reevaluate things, that's all."

"In what way?"

His smile was small and bitter. "They're closing the hotel."

"That can't come as much of a surprise though, can it? I mean, the place is about two decades past its prime, at least. We've been waiting for that hammer to fall forever."

This was clearly not the response he'd hoped for, but I had more important things to do than humor him.

"I put everything into this place and just like that they decide it's done? Without so much as a word in my direction? And when it comes, it's by email. They didn't even have the courtesy to tell me in person."

"They're in Brazil, though, right?"

"Oh yes, that's right. Fucking around in the rainforest like they suddenly give a shit about the planet. My ass. You'd better believe there's some other motive. Probably angling for a tax break or cozying up to some shitheel investor. I know this place better than my own home, and now what am I supposed to do? What was the point of any of it?"

I sat forward, looked him square in the eye. "Look, I get it. Really, I do. I may not approve of how you went about it, but nobody's going to say you didn't pour your heart and soul into this place, but sometimes done is done. We haven't had a full house in all the years I've been here, and with the economy in the shitter, any investment in this place is just throwing good money after bad. You're not a fool, Jessop. You *know* this, and if they didn't pull the trigger today, they'd have done it six weeks or six months from now."

He poured himself another glass of bourbon, held the bottle out to me. It seemed important, a gesture of mending, for me to take it, and I wanted to, but couldn't. I needed my head clearer than it currently was if I were to have any hope of finding Sheri and salvaging the mess I'd made with Naomi. Clearly disappointed, he set the bottle down on the desk.

"We're not so different, you know."

"You think?" I didn't.

"We both want women we can't have. We've both built them up in our heads to be our saviors, the cure for everything that ails us, when in truth, they deserve much better than two lonely men looking to escape from themselves. We can hardly live with who we are. Why should we expect it of anyone else?"

I didn't like to admit that there might be a kernel of truth in that, but it hardly made a difference now.

"We'd destroy them if they let us. Poison them with the same darkness that's stunted us from the start."

I rose from the seat. "Jessop, I need your help with this. If Sheri's not inside the hotel, she's outside, and that's precisely where nobody should be on a night like this. Wouldn't you rather be remembered for the good thing you did tonight than your years of being a hardass?"

But Jessop was gone, his eyes as glazed as those of the sea bass mounted on the plaque above his head. "Twenty years I've been here," he said, with a cluck of his tongue. "Twenty goddamn years, and now they want to raze the place around me."

Conscious of the time I'd already wasted, I decided to leave him to his self-pity. I was halfway out the door when he said my name. Mark, this time. Not Callahan. It was one of the few times it hadn't sounded like a curse word coming out of his mouth.

"Those guests," he said. "They're the last ones who'll ever stay here."

"I know."

"Hard to believe, but probably fitting that they should all be near-death themselves." Then he added, almost casually. "Do be

97

careful, won't you? I can't quite shake the sense that they came here to turn the lights out."

* * *

I went to the breakroom to get my coat. There was nobody else in the lobby. Even the reception desk was unmanned, a development I welcomed. Even if Naomi had told him what I'd said, I wanted to believe Pete would have seen reason considering all that was happening, but I'd also witnessed truer friendships come undone for less contentious reasons than romantic envy.

At the breakroom door, I scanned the hall for any sign of Sheri, or Danny, but it was deserted. Through the tall casement window at the far end of the hall, the snow sliced diagonally through the diminished ghost of my reflection. It was getting bad out there. Even if we had been able to get through to the police, there was no way they were making it out here until the snowplows were mobilized. That made me think again of the phones. Given our location and the severity of the winter weather, we were accustomed to being cut off, but cell phone providers make provisions for emergency calls by piggybacking off other networks to put the call through. I couldn't say for sure if it was an aberration that none of us could make that call—it wasn't like we'd had to do it very often—but like so many other things over the past few hours, it felt like one.

Coming here had been a mistake, an impulse I'd followed to avoid being alone with my grief, something I couldn't outrun forever but was perfectly happy to delay. Now I was almost nostalgic for the mundane agony of ordinary bereavement.

I hurried inside the breakroom, half expecting Pete to lunge at me out of the darkness, but when the fluorescents blinked to life, they revealed an empty room. There was a cold cup of coffee on the table and an empty sandwich wrapper on the floor. The TV was on but showed nothing but static. Grabbing my peacoat from the hook on the wall by one of the small tables, I noticed that Sheri's suede and fleece overcoat was hanging on the hook next to it. If indeed she'd gone outside, she'd done it unprotected against the storm. With a moment spared to consider all the time I had spent in this room over the years, the laughs I'd shared with the staff, with people I should have called friends, if I'd ever climbed out of my own head long enough to see them that way, I made my way outside.

11

THE SNOW BLASTED ME IN SPECTRAL WAVES, pelting my face with icy needles. Somewhere beyond the hotel, I thought I heard a tree crack and fall with the sound of an ancient hinge turning. William had salted the sidewalks before leaving, and though the drifts were rapidly erasing his work, the snow here was not as deep. I followed them around the back where Buddy Keane had parked the bus. The only source of illumination here was a tall streetlamp, installed one summer after several of the staff had their cars broken into and vandalized. There were no cars here now, though, only a paved concrete lot enclosed by brick walls on three of its four sides and a railed gate topped with razorwire on the fourth. The gate was open, the front end of the old Morningstar bus bathed in the blue light from the streetlamp. The rest was in darkness.

Opposite the bus was the metal door to the kitchen where deliveries were received, and where the staff ducked out for a smoke during lulls in service. I had hoped I'd find Sheri there, sitting on the single concrete step, huddled against the cold, but no such luck.

Disappointed, I instead turned my attention to the bus.

This close I could see it was indeed an old Volkswagen, the faded paint flaking away in patches, the Morningstar logo slowly succumbing to rust. Unlike city buses, the vehicle did not have a folding pneumatic door, just a regular one with an old metal handle. I couldn't see through the snow and ice on the windows. Could she be in there? It would have made perfect sense as a place to shelter if there hadn't been a dead guy in it.

She's not there. Go back inside. Don't think what you're thinking.

And what *was* I thinking?

I was thinking of Atkins.

I was thinking of my grandmother.

I was thinking about what happens when we die.

I was thinking about an old man forsaken on a cold bus in the middle of nowhere and the chance that some small part of him was still there.

And I was thinking that Keane's story had seemed contrived.

After a few moments of inaction in which the snow found its way into my coat, I shivered and, ever conscious that I'd left Naomi alone in the bar, I grabbed the door handle. It swung open with a shriek I felt in my fillings and before I could talk myself out of it, I stepped up and onto the bus. I still don't know what possessed me to do so after going to great pains earlier to avoid that very thing. Call it instinct. Call it some atavistic impulse, but *something* more powerful than simple curiosity pulled me toward that bus. And while it was a relief to be out of the storm, I realized I hadn't thought to bring a light and my phone was dead. "Fuck." Then I remembered the hundreds of times I'd stood outside that back kitchen door with Naomi, specifically all the times she'd forgotten her lighter, and the day she handed me one to keep for her so I could, in this regard at least, be her savior in times of need.

Aware that I was standing inside a bus with a dead man while doing everything in my power not to think of him suddenly coming back to life and rushing me, I dug a hopeful hand into my pocket. There was every chance Naomi had taken the lighter earlier. She knew it was there and never seemed to have her own.

My fingers touched the small plastic cylinder and I withdrew it, held up the lighter and whispered my thanks to whatever deity might be responsible for the break in my bad luck.

It won't work, my cynicism countered, and I flicked the wheel, saw sparks, then a long plume of flame rose before my eyes, casting a much-needed warm glow around the interior of the cold dark vehicle. The fog of my breath passed through it, dimming the light and I held it away from my face.

After a moment spared to allow my eyes to adjust, I turned and held the lighter out before me, the hissing of the gas the only sound other than my labored breathing. I was cold and damp and didn't want to be here long, but again that irresistible pull tugging me further along the path. Thinking back on it, I wonder if it had been Buddy Keane's insistence that we store the body in the hotel that stuck in my craw. Sure, leaving poor Mr. Atkins out here wasn't ideal for anyone, but in the thick of a major snowstorm, who was going to know? And if preservation of the corpse was a concern, with the thermometer hovering around the zero mark, the temperature variation between the inside of the bus versus Danny's refrigerator was bound to be negligible. It sure as hell felt like it.

I was stalling.

I shook off the internal debate in favor of action and lowered the lighter so I could see whatever was there to be seen above it.

The rows of single seats were empty but for the shadows woven by the light through the frosted windows. I counted ten seats total, five on either side, all of them in various states of disrepair.

The bench seat beneath the back window was also empty. This was where I'd expected to see Mr. Atkins lying, perhaps covered in a sheet, but that's not how I found him.

The bus shook in the grip of the wind and I was struck with the dreadful image of the fragile vehicle being blown over on its side leaving me pinned between the dead man and the window.

I drew closer, feeling as if I were about to step into an icy lake on a winter's day, an impression aided by the trickling of melting snow down the back of my neck.

Mr. Atkins sat on the floor with his back against the bench seat, as if he'd come back to life and had managed only to get his feet beneath him before collapsing again. His head was thrown back like he'd dozed off from the effort. The old man's hands were hooked into claws, as if he'd died in pain so extreme his fingers had not relaxed even after the life left him. They were dug into the legs of a pair of tweed trousers that had probably been the height of fashion thirty years before I was born. One of his neatly polished shoes had fallen off and lay upside down on the floor next to the seat. Argyle-clad toes, stiffened in death, pointed at the ceiling. The by-now-familiar amulet gleamed in the light.

Who are you people?

And then there was the smell. Not death or decomposition. That wouldn't have made any sense no matter what my imagination tried to tell me, because it was cold and Atkins hadn't been dead even a full day.

It was the smell of apples, sickly and sweet, and stronger the closer I got to the old man's body.

I felt panic surge up my chest. I wanted to be sick, wanted to scream, wanted to run, but the same compulsion that had drawn me here, the nagging voice that had demanded I come see what needed to be seen so that I might better understand whatever needed to be understood, anchored me in place.

But I did not understand what I was being shown.

I have tried over the years to forget the thing I saw growing from Mr. Atkin's mouth, but so prominently does it feature in my nightmares, it's likely to stay with me until I die. Nor is it easy to describe except to say that it looked like someone made of mottled sticks had lived inside of the old man and died trying to get out. When I leaned in with the light, almost screaming when his shadow ducked away from the flame, I saw that his jaw hung slack on its hinges, dislocated by the force of the thing that had shoved its way up his throat and out into the air.

It was a hand made of interwoven branches, the fingers a latticework of twigs and ivy tapering to points to resemble fingertips. The hand was splayed, as if in desperation, or perverse greeting. The palm was a network of twigs and snared amid this patchwork was a tangle of black hair. His eyes were dark holes refusing the light. I couldn't tell if it was mere shadow or if they were missing. One last look at the twisted mesh of sticks and vines swirling up out of the old man's distended throat and bile flooded my mouth. I doubled over and vomited a burning acidic stream onto the floor of the bus. "Jesus Chri—" I moaned, the last word drowned by another wave of nausea. I threw up until there was nothing left in my stomach and my knees felt like jelly.

I couldn't look at him, didn't know how to process what I'd seen. It made no sense. The part of me committed to retaining my mental faculties suggested it was special effects, an utterly preposterous idea considering the circumstances. Anyone who thought turning a dead man's body into an art installation was a worse threat than—

—than what? What was the implication here?

I pocketed the lighter, burning my fingers, and sank down into one of the seats so that I had some meager buffer between me and the corpse. Instinct wanted me out of there, yesterday, but I needed to collect myself. The storm was in my head now, obscuring everything, bleaching the features from the things that needed focus. It was chaos, my stomach rolling in sympathy with my thoughts like cargo jarred by the pummeling of a turbulent sea.

I quit trying to divine sense from all that had happened. Instead, I laid the facts out as they came to me. I could draw all the conclusions I wanted later. For now, just listing them would have to be enough until the capacity for analysis returned:

They came here without anyone to look after them.

No, not true. They had Keane. He might not have been an official caretaker, but he had the capability if needed.

He'd wanted the body stored in the hotel. Why?

He wanted to plant it there.

For what? What would it have done, and why isn't it doing it now?

How do you know it isn't?

That was enough to inspire movement. Grabbing the back of the seat in front of me, I jerked myself up and back out into the aisle. Using the headrests for stability, I eased myself forward, the skin on the back of my neck crawling with the certainty that Mr. Atkins was going to get up, perhaps under the power of whatever it was that had burst forth from his mouth.

The amulets. Even an idiot could put together that hand and the tree depicted in the jewelry. Keane mentioned a church. Morningstar. A cult? If so, was this some kind of ritual?

It all kept coming back to Buddy Keane.

Had they come here to die?

I reached the front of the bus, and Dorothy's words to me in the bar, her eyes so full of pain and apology came back to me once more.

I'm so sorry for what they're going to do to you.

No. Whatever they had come here to do was a lot more than just some end-of-the-road death trip. It involved *us*.

I didn't want to look back, not into the dark, but I had to, if only to be sure the dead man wasn't standing there weaving on his feet right behind me, that hand closing the distance between us and snapping at the air in front of my face.

The body was still there, sitting at the back of the bus, but I wouldn't feel fully safe until I was out of there., or at least, as safe as it was possible to feel after all that had occurred.

Was it possible I was overreacting? Could I trust myself to believe the evidence of a mind buckled by untended grief? The loss of a loved one is devastating and debilitating. It can break you. Could that be what was happening now? Was I losing it? Despite the alarming ramifications of such a development, in that moment I'd have preferred them over the alternative.

There came a sigh I might have thought was the wind, had it not come from inside the bus.

Specifically, the *back* of the bus.

It was followed by a creak, as of a wet rope being cinched tighter, and I looked just long enough to see the hand growing from the old man's mouth reach down to grab hold of his upturned chin. And then *pull*. With a cry, I ran, and tried not to hear the crunch of what my terrified mind told me was a human head being torn free of its neck, tried not to fall as I yanked the door open and fell sprawling out into the snow. And finally, tried not to scream as a ghost floated toward me through the snow.

But as I struggled to my feet, paralyzed by horror, everything in me telling me to run toward the road and just keep running until I was as far from here as it was possible to get, I saw that it was not a ghost after all.

It was Sheri.

12

H URRY," I SAID, AS SHE ENTERED THE ENCLOSURE, and nodded toward the kitchen door. "If Leigh's still inside we can get in this way. Are you all right?" I was yelling just so I couldn't hear the clamor of my own thoughts, which were a mishmash of panicked exclamations (*there are monsters here you have to run something is wrong save Naomi*) and dire predictions (*there's nowhere to run they came here because you couldn't escape you are all going to die.*) I hurried to the back door and pounded hard on the metal. "Leigh, open up!" I thought of all the reasons she might not be there to answer, from the banal to the horrific, and my stomach turned again. My plan was only to get inside, gather everyone together, and somehow get us to safety even if it meant risking the roads by car or the *very* worst-case scenario, on foot.

And the guests?

The *cult?* The same people who had, for reasons that would ever only make sense to them, jammed a tree branch down a dead guy's throat, assuming that hadn't been what killed him in the first place? *Those* people?

To hell with them. Let their god save them.

What if we abandon them and it turns out they were nothing more than they appeared to be: a group of old people on a leisurely seaside visit?

Well, they'd traveled all this way by themselves, hadn't they? They'd be fine until the morning. And if trouble arose, Jessop or Keane could look after them. The hotel was warm and full of food. It wouldn't be like we'd be leaving them helpless.

The plan, such as it was, was as ambitious as it was problematic.

I was acting out of fear and the instinct that a trap had slowly been closing around us since the guests first arrived, but without knowing more, instinct was not enough. All I had for proof to back up my insane claim was the veiled threats from one old woman, and a note saying GET AWAY from another and whatever had happened to Sheri. All that left was the thing on the bus, and I couldn't let anyone see that for themselves without putting them in peril. So, what was I going to say? And what did I *really* know?

And how much have you had to drink?

Naomi would believe me. I knew she would. Even if she didn't, she'd go along with it because she trusted me. Pete would go along with it because Naomi had, and if he knew what I'd said to her in the bar, there was no way he'd want us alone. The others? Leigh and Danny would jump at the chance to leave, even if it meant going along with a wild story from a guy who hadn't properly grieved the death of his grandmother and was now seeing monsters. Jessop was out. Despite his misgivings about the guests—and by now, I had to think everyone was feeling weirded out without knowing why—he was not going to leave the hotel, not now that he knew his time there was coming to an end.

Everything made sense and nothing did, and I thought I might be sick again.

I realized I'd been so focused on gaining access to the hotel, I hadn't taken the time to check on Sheri now that she had closed the gap between us. I turned, and she was smiling, looking herself up and down as if trying on a new outfit.

"Don't I look pretty?" she asked, and I was about to ask what she meant when she raised her head and I saw the low burning fire in her eyes. In my analysis of events, I'd forgotten *that* peculiarity. "Well," she said, flexing her fingers and inspecting them with a childish glee. "I think it fits just right, and by God, they've never felt so good."

With her other hand, she plucked at the base of her neck where the flesh had gathered, and I saw she wasn't entirely correct. And when that dawned on me, it was as if a key had turned in the lock and all the horror came flooding out. It was there in the way her right eye drooped, as if she'd suffered a stroke since I'd last seen her. It was in the way she reached up and adjusted her hairline like it was nothing more than a wig. It was in the awful way she shimmied and shuddered to fit into a body that until recently, hadn't been hers. And it was in those eyes, those terrible eyes, flickering like lanterns in a dark room.

"Do you know how long it's been since my eyes were so clear?" She was at the step now, smiling up at me, and I could see her teeth were moving like small white stones in the liquid river of her unfinished gums. I thought of the woman I'd seen in the lobby with the walker and the cloudy eyes, and before the scream could choke me, I turned and there was a face floating in front of me. This time, there was no restraining my surprise, but when I saw it was Leigh, I shoved her roughly back into the kitchen and slammed the door shut behind me hard enough to make her jump.

"Jesus Christ, Mark. What's going on?"

"How do we lock this door?"

"Was that Sheri out th—?"

"How do we lock the fucking *door?*" It was a question I'd never needed to ask because I'd used it a thousand times, but in the panic of the moment, I couldn't for the life of me figure out what to do to make sure it stayed shut.

"Pull the handle up."

I did, and then pressed my ear against the metal, listening.

"What's going on?"

I raised a hand to silence her.

"Mark?"

Heard nothing outside but the wind.

"Talk to me."

And then flinched away from the door as Sheri began to slowly drag her nails down the other side of it. "Won't you let me in? I'm cold," I heard her mumble.

"The fuck is going on?" Leigh asked, her face pale.

"Come with me." I brushed past her, headed for the door to the hall.

"Where are we going?"

"The bar."

"Mark, you're freaking me out. What happened to Sheri. Where's Danny?"

By then we were out in the hall. I looked toward the lobby. At the desk, Pete saw me and raised his hands questioningly. I could only hope he was inquiring about the current situation. Anything else could wait. I held up an index finger to indicate we'd be with him presently, then turned and headed into the bar, Leigh right behind me.

"I don't know," I told her. "But we'll find him, and then we're all getting the fuck out of here."

Someone had shut the doors to the bar. If they were locked too, I decided I was going to kick them in, and to hell with the consequences. I pushed down the handles on both and they opened easily before me, but as they swung wide, I thought my heart would explode from the dread of what I was going to see.

She'll be laid out on the bar, maybe unconscious, maybe dead, and the guests will be arguing over who gets to wear her like a fucking Halloween costume. Maybe they'll be arguing over who gets to shove a fucking branch down her throat, and if that happens, you may as well let them take you over too, because you'll never find a better way to escape the guilt of letting her die.

The room was almost as I'd left it, but only the Black man with the cane remained, and as I watched, he looked in my direction, and slowly rose from his seat. I didn't like not knowing where the others might have gone, though if I was right about what was happening tonight, at least one of them had attacked and taken over Sheri. *Taken over Sheri?* Even in my mind, it sounded insane, but how else could I explain what I'd seen on the bus and outside the back door? I had no name for what these people were, but they weren't human, or if they had been, they weren't anymore. That it all sounded crazy didn't make it any less plausible.

Naomi was not in the bar.

"Mark, will you tell me what the hell is going on?"

I turned, looked into her wide and frightened eyes. "If I tell you, you won't believe me, and if you don't believe me, you'll die." I made to push past her, but she jammed a hand in my chest, stopping me cold. Anger supplanted worry, her eyes flashing a warning that we she was not someone to be dismissed when it came to the well-being of those she loved, or any other time, for that matter.

"Give me the short version."

So I did, and as I feared, it made me sound like a raving lunatic. I watched Leigh carefully for that judgment to cross her face, but if it was there at all, she hid it well. Instead, she turned and started toward the lobby. "I'm going to find Danny."

"Good idea, but we should stay together."

"Then you'd better keep up."

When we got to the lobby, Sheri was standing at the front door with her back to us, staring out at the snow, effectively blocking the exit. She must have come around the front while I'd been telling Leigh what I knew.

"I could play in it now, if I wanted to," Sheri marveled, apparently to herself. "First time in thirty years my fingers don't burn when I make a fist. I could build a snowman or go sledding and not worry about breaking my bones. Why, I could make snow angels, though that probably wouldn't be very smart. She might not care for angels. There's so much I can do now that I couldn't before. I hardly know where to start." She fingered the amulet around her neck. "Demeter, I am your eternal servant."

"Sheri?" Leigh said and made to go to her.

I grabbed her arm. "Don't."

The summons got Sheri's attention. She looked back over her shoulder at us, her eyes black but for the tiny amber stars.

"Okay, what the fuck," Leigh blurted, and I didn't need to restrain her any longer.

"It's a miracle," Sheri said, smiling broadly. "An absolute miracle after such a long life spent not believing in them. Callum was right though. We should have believed in him from the start. The orchard is the gateway to salvation. And all we had to do was eat the seeds. Look! Do you see me?" She did a curiously child-like twirl and laughed in delight, and then brought a hand to her throat, startled by the sound. Her eyes filled with tears. "I am so very blessed."

Leigh had seen enough. She stalked across the lobby and down the first-floor hallway, calling Danny and thumping a fist on the room of every door. Inside the breakroom, we found Pete hunched over the table and spooning noodles into his mouth from a plastic container. He looked up, surprised, and choked down a bite before composing a smile. "Hey you guys, what's—?"

Leigh kept going. I lingered behind just long enough to tell Pete he needed to leave the food and come with us.

"Where are we going?"

Then I followed Leigh.

We had almost reached the stairs at the end of the hall, when behind us, someone started whistling.

"Leigh, wait," I said, but she ignored me and headed upstairs. I heard her thudding across the landing, crying out her husband's name. I did not yet know what had become of him, but prayed he was safe and that they found each other, as I hoped to find Naomi.

I looked back the way we'd come. Pete appeared in the breakroom doorway, frowning.

Behind him, The Man with the Cane was slowly making his way toward him.

"Pete," I said in a low voice. "You need to get your ass over here right now."

His perplexed look deepened, and then he turned to look at the old man. "Hello, sir. Is everything all right?"

His manners were going to get him killed or whatever the alternative was when the guests got through with you.

"A word, young man, if you wouldn't mind," said the old man, drawing out every word and twirling his cane like Charlie Chaplin. "'About the air conditionin' in my room. Like a sauna in there."

"Oh, you'd need to talk to maintenance about that and they're not here right now. Maybe crack a window?"

I'd thought a lot of crazy shit in the past half hour, but I was utterly convinced in that moment that The Man with the Cane intended to do Pete harm. I didn't want to go anywhere near that old man, but I didn't want him near Pete either.

Why not?

The insidiousness of that small mental whisper sucked the breath from me, and though I tried to resist, it found the weakness and exploited it.

What if you did nothing? Wouldn't it be the best way to know what you're dealing with? Forewarned is forearmed and all that. It might be an awful thing to see, but you've already seen enough awful things to last a lifetime, haven't you? What's one more? And then when it's all over? Why, poor Naomi will need you more than ever, just like you've always needed her.

"Couldn't get 'er open," the old man said, twirling the cane. *Swish.* He was close now, much too close for me to have any hope of getting Pete away from him.

"Pete," I said, my voice cracking on his name.

He gave me his trademark *wait-a-minute* finger.

Fuck.

"I could give you a hand. What room are you in?" he asked.

"Seven," the old man replied. "Right down there near where your friend is standin' lookin' worried."

Pete looked back at me.

"Naomi's in trouble," I said. It was the only thing I could think of to motivate him.

"What's wrong? Where is she?"

"She's here. In the room." I indicated the closed door beside me: Number 6.

Pete started to walk in my direction, much too slowly.

"*Run*," I implored.

GET AWAY.

Baffled, he quickened the pace just enough to pacify me.

Over his shoulder, the low-lying light appeared in the old man's eyes. Pete was almost clear of him, and but none of the tension left me.

There are monsters here.

"What's wrong with Naomi?"

The old man kept coming, but at least Pete was away from him.

"Hello, sir," Pete said, the professional courtesy back in his tone. I froze at the realization that he was talking to someone standing *behind* me, someone I hadn't seen coming down the stairs because my attention had been locked on Pete and his dangerous guest.

I moved away and pressed my back against the wall so I could see both guests. Mine—I had come to think of them in possessive terms, because given the intensity of their focus, it made sense to think the guests might each been *assigned* a member of staff to take over—was the old man with the oxygen mask, and though he was sucking on it, the tank to which it should have been connected was nowhere in sight, nor was the cart he'd used to carry it around. Worse, when he put the mask to his smiling mouth, more than just his breath could be seen through it. There were roots in there, fluttering against the transparent plastic whenever he exhaled.

13

IKE LEIGH BEFORE HIM, IT TOOK FOR PETE to notice the lights in the guests' otherwise dark eyes for him to accept that something wasn't right, but he hadn't heard my story, and so did not quite know what to make of what he was seeing.

I wished I had thought to bring any kind of weapon, but things had happened much too quickly for me to think of arming myself, and I still hadn't quite accepted it all. If I woke up in the morning strapped to a bed in a mental ward, it would not have come as a surprise. *Poor kid*, the doctor would say. *Lost his grandmother, then his mind.*

"I'd like to ease your mind, young man," said The Man with the Cane, and for one terrible moment, I thought he had read my thoughts. But it was not me he was addressing. He regarded Pete as a hungry dog might a sirloin. That it was *only* Pete holding his interest lent weight to my theory about the guests each being assigned a single target. It made sense. If their objective was to infiltrate younger, healthier bodies, why would they need more than one? "I'd like to tell you this is all quick n' painless, that once it's over you go to a better place, but I have no way of knowin' that and don't rightly believe it's proper to lie to someone in their final hour about what's comin' next."

There it was. The plain and simple truth, delivered as a death warrant.

"What is he talking about, bro?" Pete asked.

To my right, the old man with the mask simply stared at me.

"Pete," I muttered.

He'd had the good sense to back up to the wall beside me. Even if he didn't understand what was happening, he'd accepted it as odd, and possibly lethal. If he survived, he could ponder the logic of it all for the rest of his natural life. Right now, his instinct had taken over, and he looked scared to death.

"What?"

I didn't know much more than he did about what this process, this takeover, entailed. I hadn't seen it happen, but I did know the elderly, having been raised by a woman who was sixty-three when she took me in, and gambled on them being hard of hearing and none too spry. In the face of the supernatural, I had forgotten the frailty of the natural, and that offered a glimmer of hope. Once they took over their younger hosts, however, we'd be equally matched, not to mention the difficulty involved in trying to fight off something wearing the face of someone you know.

With Sheri—or whomever Sheri was now—by the main entrance, I had to assume that someone else had installed themselves in the kitchen to block the delivery door. We could attempt to rush either one, but that left us out in the cold. A more sensible option might be to get to one of the vacant rooms and wait this out, or hole up there until we could formulate a more cohesive plan. The Windcrest didn't have connecting rooms, so there would only be the one entry to defend.

In a whisper just forceful enough to be heard over the wind battering against the window behind Oxygen Man, I told Pete: "On three. Run for the stairs."

"I don't understand what's happening."

"It'll be all right. Just stay close to me."

"Now what are you little piggies whisperin' about, I wonder?" said The Man with the Cane.

"We're figuring out the best way to deal with your window," I said.

Pete kept his eyes on him. "What about Naomi?"

"I don't know where she is, but we'll find her."

"But you said—"

"I know what I said. Forget it, okay? Just get to the stairs. Ready?"

"No."

"One..."

Movement in the lobby. It was Sheri, waltzing, humming that peculiar song the guests had been singing in the bar.

The Man with the Cane stepped closer, the light in his eyes flaring like lit matches.

"Two." Oxygen Man's breath quickened, those tendrils skittering in feverish anticipation against the mask. It made the sound of a crab trapped in a plastic bucket.

"Three." Shoulders hunched, body tensed, I broke away from the wall in a run, my elbow ramming into Oxygen Man's ribs. He grunted and staggered away from me, the mask forgotten, and I caught a brief glimpse of those roots whipping and snapping at the air above his mouth as fire raged from his eyes.

Heart hammering in my chest, I didn't look back until I heard Pete cry out.

He was on the floor, the crook of the old man's cane hooked around his ankle.

"Now where you goin' in such a hurry, boy? We've got business, you and I. Or is it you and me? I forget."

Screaming, Pete grabbed at the carpet, trying to crawl free. He kicked his legs out behind him and connected with his captor's jaw. There was an awful crunch and the lower half of the old man's face crumbled away as if it had been made of compacted dirt, his dentures clacking to the floor.

Despite my earlier indecision, I wanted desperately to go back and save Pete, but as soon as I took a step, Oxygen Man blocked my path. His eyes were like miniature suns. Beneath the raw red impressions caused by the edges of mask, now lying forgotten on the floor, roots tumbled from his mouth like worms. They whipped and lashed and as I looked on in horror, they wove themselves together into the shape of a hand. It reached for me, and though I dared not look, I knew the same thing was happening to Pete. His scream was low and hoarse and turned my blood to ice.

I wanted to shove the old man away from me, but his skin had a vague translucence to it now that made me fear my hands would plunge into him, expediting his assimilation of me.

There was nowhere to go but upstairs.

So that's what I did, but not before seeing The Man with the Cane drop to his knees, the hand bursting forth from his mouth to penetrate the back of Pete's skull.

Guts in turmoil, I ran.

14

H IS DEATH WOULD HAUNT ME FOR THE REST of my life, but there would be ample time for recriminations later, to think of all the things I could have done, and to wonder if I'd really wanted to. For now, I needed to find Naomi, Leigh, and Danny, assuming any of them had made it this far.

The first thing I saw when I reached the second floor was a walker overturned outside the open door of Room 12. The owner had collapsed in the doorway, but only her stockinged feet were visible. I imagined her summoning Sheri on the pretense of being lost on the second floor and taking her once they were alone.

Overhead, the lights flickered, and I prayed the power would hold. In darkness, we'd be doomed.

I did not check to see if the old woman was still alive. She lived in Sheri now and all I would see if I inspected the body was another vile perversion of natural biology, some unholy fusion of nature and flesh. What I couldn't keep from wondering, however, was where Sheri, the *real* Sheri, had gone once the transfer was complete. Did she simply cease to exist, dead in the final sense of the word, or was her mind a prisoner, screaming to get out? This last was too terrible a thing to contemplate, so I chose to believe she'd found peace.

Expecting the Oxygen Man to appear at the top of the stairs at any moment, a development which I'd decided would end with his death over my own, I moved quickly from room to room.

I found Danny in Room 17, the last room before the stairs to the third floor.

He was sitting on the edge of the bed with his back to me, head lowered, hugging himself tightly and moaning. Cautiously, I edged into the room and gently rapped a knuckle against the door. "Danny? Hey man, you okay? Where's Leigh?"

He stopped rocking back and forth but did not turn to acknowledge me.

"I'm not going to expect you to understand," he said, and his accent was not his own. "And if you decide to punish me for my sins, I won't stop you. I won't even look."

It was the Asian guest.

I sagged against the door and put my hand over my eyes.

"Six years," he said, voice wavering. "I could not go home to see my sister. She is sick. She could not come. And me, useless, too old, could not take a plane because of my lungs. They said it was too dangerous. I should have tried. I wanted to. Then the church opened in Morningstar. I thought I might ask God for help, ask him for a miracle. But the god of that church was not the one I have worshipped all my life. It was not a god at all, but they said it would make my wishes come true if I promised to believe. I did not come here to hurt anyone. I want you to believe that."

I didn't say anything. I just listened, wishing I could wake up back in the world where none of this was possible, where the laws of the universe still held true.

"Do you know how hard it is being away from your family?" he asked me. "Maybe you do."

Yes, I do.

"I put myself in the home because I started to forget things. I would leave the gas on and the neighbors would call the police. I would forget to put the trash out and the house would fill with roaches. I would walk down the street and suddenly forget I lived there. I would forget I was no longer young and in love with a beautiful wife to come home to. Do you know what that's like? To feel the agony of loss over and over again, to have your heart broken into a million pieces because you forgot you're alone? There is greater dignity in death than growing old and forgetting your reasons for living. *They* promised to give it back to me. Maybe I am weak for agreeing, but I don't know any man who would have refused. I wanted my life back. What would *you* have done?"

I took a step into the room, which revealed enough for me to see the body on the floor next to where Danny sat. The suspenders and the snazzy yellow tie.

"And you think if you go to a home, they will take care of you and things will be better. You'll be with people who understand. With friends. But then a virus comes and people blame China, and it doesn't matter if you're Korean, you look different enough for them to treat you badly. Why would I not have wanted to start again with a different face? It has never been easy for me. This world has not been kind."

Someone grabbed my shoulder and my heart leapt into my throat. I spun, ready to attack, sure it was Oxygen Man come to finish what he'd started, to shove those roots into my mouth and take my body over while his eyes blazed into mine, watching as my soul turned to ash.

It was Leigh. I backed away from her, momentarily unsure I could trust that it was really her, but then noticed how pale she was and that her mascara was smudged, eyes red and swollen from crying. Normal *human* eyes. If there was any truth to Shakespeare's adage about the eyes being the windows to the soul, then perhaps the blackness in theirs meant the guests occupied us at the expense of their own souls. If that didn't abate with time, I couldn't see how they expected to infiltrate society. Humankind can be oblivious at the best of times, but black eyes with glowing lights in them are hard to ignore.

Leigh did not react with surprise to the sight of Danny on the bed which meant she had already been here and had seen what had become of him. I wanted to say something, to offer some measure of comfort, but then remembered my ambivalence toward the mourners at Magda's funeral and said nothing instead.

"Is there any chance he's still in there?" she asked.

"I don't know."

She put a hand on my arm and wordlessly guided me back to the door, ushering me out of the room. I expected her to follow, but she stayed inside while the man pretending to be her husband continued his lament.

"This is not what I wanted. Nothing is worth taking the life of another man just so I can fulfil my own selfish desires," he continued, oblivious to the silent film playing out in the room behind him. "I only wish now that I could take it back, to somehow atone for what I've done." He began to weep, and something broke inside me. I thought of them as monsters, but the man sitting on the bed, though he had taken a life that wasn't his to take, did it for no more wicked a reason than to get back the things age had denied him. I wanted to hate him for that and couldn't.

As Leigh shut the door on me, her eyes met mine. "Naomi's on the third floor. Room 21."

She had a pipe wrench in her hand.

KEALAN PATRICK BURKE

15

THERE HADN'T BEEN TIME TO CONSIDER what would happen once this was all over. Assuming we made it out alive, I couldn't imagine any of us doing what other people do every single day: get on with our lives in the wake of death. The idea seemed ridiculously farfetched. My own refusal to sit down with my grief over Magda and look it in the face was not a positive indication of what awaited me. Weeks, months, or years from now, the black wave would come to wash all the good from my life, long after I'd convinced myself the tide had gone out. Worse, we would not be leaving here knowing some terrible evil had been conquered. Even if we'd been the kind of people who could go floor to floor murdering the monsters who'd taken our friends, who was to say it ended here, or that the church of which Buddy Keane spoke was an anomaly? After all, how many religions limit themselves to a single chapter in a retirement home? And even if we did manage to kill the guests, they looked to us like our friends, and that's also how they'd look to the police.

It would be the ultimate irony to survive this night only to spend the rest of my life in prison wishing I'd let Oxygen Man have what he'd come here to take. Something told me, however, that the same problem would not exist with the original bodies of the guests. Judging by what I'd seen on the Morningstar bus and the way the man with the cane's jaw had crumbled like shale, I suspected there would be nothing to find once this night was over. In fact, I doubted very much that there would be any record of the guests at all. The Korean man's tearful confession told me that, once the storm passed, visitors to the hotel would find it empty, because even though they could pass as us, the guests had no intention of sticking around. No counterfeit Pete on reception or Sheri on housekeeping. No fake Danny in the kitchen. Part of the problem was that unless their takeover was complete and all of us were assimilated, the others couldn't get away with their façade. We'd all need to be part of the ruse. And how good could that ruse possibly be unless they retained the skills and habits and mannerisms of those they inhabited? Which, if Danny's Korean accent was anything to go by, they did not. No, they didn't come all this way to pull off a heist only to install themselves in the very place they'd robbed. They had objectives, stories of their own that needed final chapters, though thanks to Leigh, the Asian man's story, at least, would remain unfinished.

Despite the suffocating sense that I was being watched and that at any moment, one of the doors on the third floor would fly open and I'd meet my premature end, my walk to Naomi's room went unchallenged.

When I reached the door, I thought of knocking, of announcing myself, just in case she decided to greet my intrusion with a hammer to the face, but then I considered how much she was likely to know about what was happening in the hotel. Maybe she thought, as any rational person would, that Sheri was still missing and that was the worst of our problems. How was I going to tell her otherwise? And how was I supposed to tell her what had happened to the man she loved?

A shuffling on the stairs.

Cones of amber light split the darkness in the stairwell.

Quietly, I turned the handle and let myself into Naomi's Room.

16

WHEN I STEPPED INSIDE AND LOCKED THE DOOR behind me, my shoe crunched down on broken glass. Someone had toppled the bureau, shattering the attached mirror. The mattress had been flipped off the bed to form a vertical and possibly accidental blockade over the room's only window. Multicolored stains blossomed on the underside and rusted metal barbs poked through the skin of the box spring. The cheap painting of a summertime meadow had been ripped off the walls, the canvas punctured and spotted with blood. The TV had been thrown to the floor, but the screen appeared to be intact. The cheap coffee maker was in pieces.

"Naomi?"

There were only two rooms: the main room and the bathroom. The bathroom door was shut and there was a smear of blood above the handle. I cocked my head, listening for some sound of movement, pleading with whatever god might be tuned in to the hotel's station tonight that I would not find a body in there, or if I did, that it was not the girl I loved.

I stepped over the glass and around the TV, and the bathroom door handle moved.

I froze, then jumped as someone rapped a knuckle on the other door. Oxygen Man, I assumed, and was thankful I'd thought to lock it.

The storm pressed against the windows hard enough to make the broken glass vibrate on the floor.

At length, the bathroom door opened.

And Naomi came out.

17

MY PLAN TO ESCAPE MY LIFE HAD NEVER been about independence, or this town, or new beginnings. I'd been trying to escape myself and that's something you only get to outrun at the very end of your story. It shouldn't have taken the intervention of the horrors I'd encountered at Windcrest for me to truly see it, but now that it was laid bare before me, I knew I would never leave Miriam's Cove because it was where I belonged.

I loved Naomi. It was not something I'd planned or did on purpose. It wasn't like I hadn't tried to talk myself out of it in all the time I'd known her. I'd dated other people, but I would never love anyone quite the same way. I can't even tell you why.

But when she emerged from the bathroom, her eyes wide with shock, skin streaked and spotted with blood, a long shard of mirror glass held so tightly in her hand, it had cut through her palm, all I wanted to do was protect her for as long as she would let me.

And in the end, she didn't speak at all. Neither of us did. She simply walked to me, threw her arms around my neck, and hugged me so tightly it hurt. Over her shoulder I could see the bathroom mirror through the open door.

The shower curtain had been pulled off the rails and was draped over a body sitting upright in the tub.

18

WE WALKED LIKE BLAST VICTIMS THROUGH THE ROOM to the door. Oxygen Man—if that's who'd been out there—hadn't knocked again, but that was no guarantee that he wasn't waiting for us, but when I moved to shield Naomi from view, she shook her head, reached past me, and opened the door, the shard of glass in hand. Whatever had happened in this room had changed her, as it must, just as this night would change all it touched.

She opened the door and peered out, then moved slowly out into the hall. I followed. There was no sign of Oxygen Man, but Leigh was sitting on the top step of the stairs looking down onto the second-floor landing. We approached her with caution, the shard of glass gleaming wickedly in Naomi's hand, until we were close enough to see what she was looking at.

"Fucker took a bite out of my wrist," Leigh said.

19

AS WE HEADED DOWNSTAIRS, I TRIED TO DO THE MATH: The woman with the walker had taken over Sheri. If it was safe to assume they became less of a threat as soon as they got what they wanted, as evidenced by her dancing and the Korean man's guilt, then we could also cross of The Man with the Cane too. Leigh had killed the Korean and Oxygen Man, and Naomi had killed one too.

"Which one of them attacked you?" I asked. We were passing the elevator on the second floor, Leigh trailing behind and cradling her bloody wrist.

The pained expression told me this event was not something Naomi wanted to talk about, now, perhaps ever.

"It's important," I added.

"I don't know her name," she said quietly. "She had purple hair. Her mouth...She...she tried to..."

I put my arm around her and told her it was going to be okay, a ridiculous promise even if we made it out of here alive.

Agnes.

Which, if I had it right, left only Dorothy and the Bearded Man with the bad skin. As far as I knew, Leigh was the only one who hadn't yet had one of them attempt to take her over, so one could assume she was Dorothy's intended target. That might be a good thing, considering how resistant Dorothy had shown herself to be in the bar. Of course, that had been earlier, and a lot had changed since then. Thus, by process of elimination, The Bearded Man's target was Jessop.

It had been a while since I'd thought of the manager. It wasn't as if his presence would have helped in any way. Even if he'd witnessed the unnatural events tonight, I wasn't fully convinced he wouldn't have stayed behind, as if he were the captain of the Titanic and not the intemperate steward of a dead hotel.

Still, while I owed him nothing, I knew I couldn't leave without alerting him to the danger. If he scoffed at me, fine, I wasn't going to endanger myself and the others trying to make him see reason any longer than I had to. All of which assumed he hadn't already fallen victim to his guest, and the odds of that were high.

But there was someone else I hadn't figured into the equation.

Buddy Keane.

And I knew why.

Before the Morningstar bus headed off on its journey from the retirement home, I'm sure Buddy Keane was who he said he was, who he had always been: a city bus driver who took short-distance gigs for the extra money, until one of the old men took him over, the same old man who was now lying at the back of that bus with a hand growing from his throat. He was there because he had taken Buddy Keane's place, leaving only a moldering husk behind. When I met him in the lobby, Buddy's eyes were red. I didn't think it anything out of the ordinary. He had driven a long way on inhospitable roads in the snow. That would make anybody's eyes sore. What I now realized was that given time, the guests' eyes returned to normal, maybe not the color of the host they'd subsumed, but good enough not to warrant a second look. Buddy's eyes had not quite completed the change.

I wondered where Buddy was now.

Halfway down the stairs to the ground floor, I held Naomi back. Leigh nodded and continued on without us, stricken and battle-scarred but ready for whatever else the night had to throw at her.

"Be careful," I said.

She hefted the bloodstained wrench and nodded solemnly. "I'm getting out of here and God help anyone who tries to stop me." Then she was gone.

Naomi, a ghost of herself, looked at me with hollow eyes.

"We need to talk about Pete," I said.

20

I HELD HER WHILE SHE WEPT, and when at last, we were ready to keep moving, she did not look at the husk of The Man with the Cane in the hall, at the twisted hand growing from his mouth, fingers reaching toward the heavens in supplication. She did not ask if he was the one who had taken Pete. She said nothing at all because it didn't matter.

Though his body might be rambling around the hotel, Pete was gone.

KEALAN PATRICK BURKE

148

21

J ESSOP ALWAYS CHOSE THE MUSIC THAT PLAYED in the hotel, and though he pretended our input was welcome, our choices never appeared on his playlist. His selections were mostly safe, inoffensive fare, innocuous enough to barely register, unless like us, you heard it on a loop all year round. James Taylor, Johnny Mathis, Neil Diamond, Kenny G, Carly Simon, The Carpenters, all the easy listening types.

The music that drew us toward the lobby now was, like all his greatest hits, piped through the speakers from the PA system in his office.

The song, however, was the strange atonal one the guests had brought with them into the hotel. I don't really know how to describe it other than to say it sounded hymnal if hymns were traditionally played at multiple speeds and with no adherence to the principles of traditional rhythm.

Naomi and I joined Leigh in watching the peculiar spectacle taking place in the lobby. The Bearded Man was sitting on the highbacked sofa near the front door, hands in his lap, eyes shut, smiling rapturously. Occasionally he reached up to scratch at the eczemic patch of skin on his cheek, but otherwise seemed lost in the music.

Dorothy stood in the alcove leading to The Ocean Room. She too seemed entranced by the song. It was the first time since her arrival that I had seen her look happy.

Pete sat behind reception, a glass of something amber in his hand. He smiled broadly and slapped his knee to keep time with the music, which to me, seemed an impossible feat given its bizarre fluctuating tempo. At the sight of him, Naomi started to tremble, but to her credit, she did not try to go to him. Perhaps it was the amulet he wore. Perhaps it was the glow in his unfinished eyes.

I had expected an assault, an ambush, chaos, a last ditch-effort by the guests to finish what they'd come here to do.

Instead, there was music, and in the center of the room under the dusty old chandeliers, Jessop waltzing with Sheri.

"I owe Danny fifty bucks," Leigh said, pain creasing her face.

"How's that?" I asked.

"He said those two would never end up together."

"They didn't."

The presence of The Bearded Man told me that Jessop hadn't been taken over. Otherwise, the former would be a husk on the floor somewhere. Which meant that, however it had come to pass, Jessop had chosen to dance with Sheri amidst the guests with the burning eyes. Had they forced him to do it for their amusement? Had he somehow fooled himself into thinking this was all some kind of game?

After watching him for a while, I didn't think so. The solution appeared to me a lot simpler than that.

Jessop had seen the guests for what they were. He knew Sheri was not herself.

He just didn't care. I'd been right in my assumption that he wouldn't leave the hotel. He couldn't. There was nothing left for him now. Nothing but the woman pretending to be Sheri.

She was in his arms, and wherever the two of them were as they swooped and turned and dipped and whirled, it was not here. There might be horror for us here, but for Jessop at least, and the guests themselves, there was magic too, a wonderful kind of impossible dream that restored to them they things they'd lost or had never had to begin with. If they took Jessop, and one had to assume they were going to, he would consider it a mercy, a release of a kind he would never be able to give himself.

Sometimes when you can't face the truth looking back at you in the mirror, lies are all you've got left.

The woman who had once been Sheri laughed and spun into Jessop's embrace, enjoying her new life and new body in the arms of a man who had never figured out how to be at home in his own.

"We should go," I said. The plan had changed abruptly after the bloodshed upstairs. I didn't want Naomi anywhere near the woman she'd killed, and the walls had started to close in on me. Sooner or later, Dorothy was going to come for Leigh. I figured even if we had to lock ourselves into a car until the snow stopped or take our chances in the storm, we'd be better off out there than in here, with *them*.

"Lead the way," Leigh said.

I did, keeping close to the window and as far away from any of the guests, and Jessop, as I could. I didn't want to meet his eyes but found I could not stop watching him. I could say that even though the guests had not taken him yet, he was still not the Jessop I knew, but then, I don't think I ever really knew the man at all, and I think that was how he wanted it.

Nobody stopped us as we made our way out through the doors, but I would not relax until they were shut behind us and we were far away from here. As I turned to close them behind me, I saw Jessop watching me over Sheri's shoulder. I saw nothing but joy on his face. He nodded at me, just once, an acknowledgement of something unknown in a night shrouded in mystery, and then turned, lost in the throes of the dance.

The cold wind whipped at our clothes and pummeled us with snowy gusts. Naomi ducked her head and I pulled her closer while Leigh trudged toward her car. Her foot collided with something buried in the snow and she cursed, kicked out at it, and then something dawned on her. She looked from the object to her car, and then around at the other vehicles, all of them hunkered silently beneath capes of snow.

"What is it?" I asked and watched as she reached down and pulled Oxygen Man's tank from the drifts.

"My hood is unlatched. I think they fucked with the cars," she said grimly.

Which made perfect sense. We wouldn't have been much use to them if we could leave at any time.

"Now what do we do?" Naomi asked, shivering in my arms.

They might have removed our way of leaving, but they wouldn't have scuttled their own.

"The bus," I said.

Leigh frowned. "We don't have the keys."

"I have a feeling we won't need them."

22

UDDY KEANE WAS SITTING IN THE DRIVER SEAT, where I assumed he'd been waiting once he realized the night was not going to go according to plan. We stood in the enclosure looking in at him.

He beckoned to us through the frosted window.

I turned to Leigh. "Keep an eye on Naomi."

"Is he, y'know, one of them?"

"I think so."

"What are you going to do?"

"Talk to him. See if there's a way out of this for all of us."

"And if there isn't?"

"Then I don't think any of us will have to worry about it for very long."

She clearly thought the plan a foolish one, but she put her arm around Naomi, who wasn't wearing a coat and looked blue with the cold, and didn't try to stop me. We were out of options now, and out of time.

I turned back to the bus.

Buddy leaned over and opened the passenger door.

23

I SHUT THE DOOR BEHIND ME. If Buddy turned out to be the architect of all this madness and morphed into the devil, I wanted the girls to have a fighting chance of running. The door of a rickety old Volkswagen bus wasn't likely to present much of an obstacle, but I felt better having it closed.

I slid into the seat across from Buddy and nearest the door.

Buddy started the engine and the heat kicked on. For this, at least, I was grateful.

"Now what?" I asked.

He shrugged. "We leave."

"Just like that."

"Unless you have unfinished business in there, I think it's best if we all move on, don't you?"

"Why?"

"Because the clock's run out. Snowplows are already clearin' the roads. The police'll have tried to call to make sure you folks are okay. It's what they do in neighborly communities like these. Eventually they'll send someone out here to check. The more people we have here, the messier things get. Besides, it's cold, and I hate the cold."

"So, you're letting us go?"

The leather creaked as he turned in his seat to look back at me. "Letting you go? Kid, you give me way too much credit. I was never keepin' you here. I'm merely a servant."

"Of what?"

He exhaled explosively. "If we have that conversation, you'll be old by the end of it."

"Try me."

He spoke while clearing the condensation from the windshield with agitated sweeps of his hand. "Fine. Are you familiar with The Myth of Pruriette's Orchard? The Seed-Sowers of Ildayne? Demeter's Rite? Did they read bedtime stories to you of the Terrible Maiden of Due South? Of the Planters of Milknoon?"

"No."

"No, of course not, because you're from here, and I don't have the time to educate you on stuff you'd never understand or know what to do with. If you're desperate for lessons, try this one: tonight, you saw the guests and they saw you. Before they came, you knew nothin' of them and even less of yourself. If that's not enough for a lifetime of wonder, you're not someone who's ever gonna see past the reach of his own hand. Besides, your story's just startin'. Plenty of answers in store for you on the road."

I sleeved a clear arc of my own in the condensation and looked out at Naomi and Leigh. "What happens to them?"

"They freeze to death if you don't let them in."

"Not the girls. The others. Pete and Danny and Sheri and Jessop. What happens to the original owner when a new tenant moves in?"

"Only they know."

"And you?"

"What about me?"

"Who are you? The old man back there on the floor?"

"Callum Atkins. Nice to meet you. Now be a good kid and let the ladies in before they catch their deaths out there."

KEALAN PATRICK BURKE

24

NONE OF US SPOKE AGAIN UNTIL THE SNOWPLOWS had finished carving their way through the night. Though Buddy Keane might have been a good bus driver, Callum Atkins, the man who currently occupied Buddy's body, was not nearly so capable and we almost ended up stalled in the drifts. "I'm more at home in a Packard," he quipped.

Eventually, with the engine protesting like a frightened calf, he got us out of there.

When we passed the front of the hotel, the lights were out, but a frail white form stood with her hands pressed against the glass of the main doors, the lights in her eyes like distant ships on a black sea.

"Don't worry about her," Buddy/Callum said. "She'll get another shot. One of the police officers is a woman. Dotty always loved to play dress-up."

"Why didn't she go through with it?"

"Some of them can't. It happens."

"What happens to them if they don't?"

"'The seed, once taken, groweth toward the sun, so the Lady can pluck the fruit from the sky.' He smiled. "In layman's terms, you can tell a tree to stop growing, but that don't mean it'll listen. They knew what they were getting' into. Most of them anyway. Myself? I had money on the Korean guy foldin' like a cheap card table. After a while you can tell. Too pure a conscience can be their undoing."

I didn't ask him any more questions, because the answers made little sense to me, and because I was tired. While I didn't trust him, I no longer felt the dread of imminent danger. Maybe it would turn out that he was driving us somewhere where three old folks were waiting for new bodies, but I didn't think so. And if that's what happened, I no longer had the strength to fight.

When we passed a cop car slowly driving in the other direction, Buddy whistled. "That right there is Dotty's last shot." While he spoke, Leigh tapped the wrench against my hand. She was sitting in the seat behind me, her eyes full of cold vengeance. I looked down at the weapon, then shook my head. Her face was a chaos of unrefined anger, but she didn't force the act upon me, nor did she try for Buddy herself.

Then, unbelievably, I dozed off, and when I awoke with a start, unsure of who I was, I saw the front door of Magda's house waiting for me in the dark. Naomi too had fallen asleep. I gently shook her awake and saw in her face the same look of confusion and wishful thinking. Then I saw the pain rush back in to drown it.

I was walking up the path with Naomi and Leigh after we made the decision to get as drunk as humanly possible before deciding how we were supposed to live in the aftermath of what we'd been through, when Buddy rolled down his window.

"Kid, c'mere," he said. I handed Naomi my keys and told them to go inside and get warm. After a moment's hesitation, they did.

I went back to the bus.

Buddy smiled. "You're young, Mark. You have your whole life ahead of you. Don't forget that. If you have any sense, you'll relish every second of it. No matter what, though..." He paused to light a cigar and then puffed blue smoke out into the frigid air. "...remember that no amount of livin' will stop you from gettin' old, and when that day comes, when your joints are stiff and everythin' hurts, and all your friends are gone, maybe then you'll meet someone like me. And maybe we can help you."

"I don't think so," I told him.

"Yeah, everyone says that in the beginning. Next thing you know, they're swallowing apple seeds from the orchard and slippin' into somethin' a little more comfortable."

He started to roll up the window and I put my hand on the glass. He paused, eyebrows raised.

"Where are you going?" I asked.

"To find myself a new suit. They'll be looking for this one." He had the window almost shut when he grinned out at me and added, "I hear the weather's nice in Florida this time of year."

I watched him pull out into the road, the wheels slipping in the slush, until there was nothing left to see but the dark.

25

PRIL WAS A MONTH OF ENDLESS RAIN. Once, that might have darkened my spirits, but things had changed in the months since my last night at the hotel. Out of respect for Peter's memory, Naomi didn't move in with me, but we started seeing a lot of each other. It wasn't romantic, not at first and not for a long time. Both of us felt that no matter how strong our connection, it was wise to ensure it hadn't been forged solely because of our experiences that night. Gradually we relaxed into each other, allowing what was there to blossom, while remaining mindful of the hallowed ground upon which our relationship was built.

Magda left me everything in her will, including a lengthy letter she had written a few weeks after her diagnosis. I won't share all of it here because it's eight pages long and it upsets me and some things I prefer to keep just for me, but one part is worth passing along, and it's this:

"Don't mourn too long because pain can make you sick. I missed Edward something fierce after he died and sometimes, I wonder if this goddamned cancer isn't just a great big knotted up ball of all that sorrow. He wasn't what anyone would call a romantic, my Eddie, and to be fair, I'm not sure I ever was either. We weren't very touchy. We didn't cuddle or call each other cute names or hold hands in public. We had more differences than things in common, but it didn't matter. We were there for each other, like those sycamores in the back yard, and I loved him, and I know he loved me too. We were solid together, and I don't regret a single moment I spent with him. Life is everything, love is too. Don't let my passing turn into your sickness, Mark. Don't let it be the roadblock you can't get around on the path to your own true love. Go out there and find it. It won't wait forever. Find it, grab it, and never look back. We don't have all the time in the world."

As expected, she left me the house and the car, and twelve thousand dollars in savings. For a while, it looked as if her estranged son in Dubai was going to challenge me for it, but when he realized it was apt to be a whole lot of trouble for such little reward, he retreated to his ivory tower and that was the end of it.

I never went back to the hotel out of fear of what might await me there, even though the day after the guests came, Jessop, Mark, and Sheri disappeared without a trace, along with the bodies of the old folk who'd infiltrated them, just as I suspected they would. They had other business to attend to, the ashes of the bodies no doubt returned to feed their orchard. It made national news for a while, and the police called upon us often, but as I wasn't scheduled to work the night in question, I simply pretended I hadn't, and nobody was there to say otherwise. Naomi's story was that she went to bed in one of the vacant rooms after her shift ended and woke up to find herself alone. She claimed to know nothing about the trashed room. It was worse for Leigh, who had to convince the cops she knew nothing of Danny's disappearance when her face betrayed every lie. What got her out of it in the end, aside from the lack of compelling evidence, was the indomitable love with which she spoke of the man she'd lost.

It lasted the better part of a year, but eventually The Windcrest story became just another mystery for true-crime buffs and the conspiracy-minded to obsess over.

Jessop vanished too, of course, and I think of him more now than I ever did when he was alive. Sometimes an old war movie will play on the TV and I'll start to choke up a bit, which never fails to surprise me. We weren't friends, and yet for some strange reason, I miss him. Perhaps it's just another kind of mourning.

The Crosses were none-too-pleased about the attention around The Windcrest in the wake of the disappearances, and I have to think that if they hadn't already planned on shutting it down, that would have forced their hand. Three months after our hellish night, they razed the place. Wish I could say I miss it.

And whatever the world thought happened there, they linked Officer Marion Daly to it because she resigned from her job with the Miriam's Cove P.D. two days later and skipped town. I guess Dorothy changed her mind, in the end.

At first, Leigh came to see us a lot, but less as time went on. Sometimes she brought the kids, sometimes she didn't. The summer after everything went down at the hotel, we barbecued steaks in the backyard and traded funny stories about Danny while drinking way more to his memory than it could hold. That day, I paid more attention to the sycamores than I had in all the years I'd lived there, particularly to the sound of the breeze rustling through the leaves and the way the dappled sunlight danced upon the grass. I'm not sure if I believe in the afterlife, though I'm a lot more open to it than I was before that night at the hotel.

For now, it will do to just live and see where the road takes us.

26

LAST NIGHT WAS OUR TWO-YEAR ANNIVERSARY together. We went to that new place down by the pier and had oysters and crab legs and champagne. Then we walked the boardwalk and held hands while the tide gurgled and lapped at the pilings.

It was one of the best nights I've ever had.

Later, as we lay in bed, we talked, not for the first time, about having kids. Naomi says she's open to it, but not yet. I can't help but feel it's her way of letting me down gently until I stop asking. That's something I will have to reconcile, but not right now. She says she wants to travel first and then maybe pursue her one true passion: acting. She said she misses it, though I don't recall ever hearing her talk about it before and can't find a period in her life in which she could possibly had given it enough time.

Then she told me she was thinking of enrolling in community theater.

I watched the shadows waltz on the ceiling and told myself she hadn't pronounced it *theatah,* or that if she had said it that way, it was just another of those funny coincidences that come along when you least expect them.

When I asked her to say it again, she laughed at me.

Though I willed them away, the memory of Agnes' words that night in The Ocean Room snaked their way back up out of my subconscious. Agnes, who'd been covered by a sheet so I couldn't see whether there was a hand crawling out of her mouth.

I have a feeling one day we're going to be very close, and I for one cannot wait.

"What's wrong, honeybear?" Naomi said, and kissed my cheek. "Your heart's racing all of a sudden."

Was that glee I heard in her voice?

What poor Dotty doesn't understand is that to truly sell a scene, you must commit to it entirely, body and soul. Otherwise, what is it other than a charade?

I hadn't seen the body clearly, had confirmed nothing at all. I'd just taken it on faith that Naomi had killed the old woman because it was the only reality I could accept and I dared not question it. Now that the long-delayed doubt had finally caught up with me, how would I ever again be sure?

Honeybear.

Naomi wore contacts. What better way to hide the effect the takeover had on their eyes?

I turned to look at her, trying to steel myself against the fear that curdled in the base of my throat.

She sat up, her face a mask of concern, and the sheet fell away, revealing her alabaster skin in the light through the bedroom window.

Then she told me she loved me.

And when I looked into her eyes, as deep into them as she would allow, I saw no sparks, no low lights, and no lies.

She smiled, and after a moment, I returned it and we lost ourselves in each other.

Because in the end, Magda was right.

Life really is everything.

Love is too.

KEALAN PATRICK BURKE

172

about the author

Hailed by Booklist as "one of the most clever and original talents in contemporary horror," Kealan Patrick Burke was born and raised in Ireland and emigrated to the United States a few weeks before 9/11. Since then, he has written five novels, among them the popular southern gothic slasher KIN, and over two hundred short stories and novellas, including BLANKY and THE HOUSE ON ABIGAIL LANE, both of which are currently in development for film and TV.

A five-time Bram Stoker Award-nominee, Burke won the award in 2005 for his coming-of-age novella THE TURTLE BOY, the first book in the acclaimed Timmy Quinn series.

As editor, he helmed the anthologies NIGHT VISIONS 12, TAVERNS OF THE DEAD, and QUIETLY NOW, a tribute anthology to one of Burke's influences, the late Charles L. Grant.

Most recently, he completed a new novel, MR. STITCH, a collection entitled GUESTS for Suntup Editions, and adapted SOUR CANDY for John Carpenter's NIGHT TERRORS series of graphic novels.

Kealan is represented by Merrilee Heifetz at Writers House and Kassie Evashevski at Anonymous Content.

He lives in an unhaunted house in Ohio with a Scooby Doo lookalike rescue named Red. Visit him on the web at www.kealanpatrickburke.com